APPLAUSE FOR THE PLAYS OF A. R. GURNEY

A. R. GURNEY is the author of many highly acclaimed plays, including *The Cocktail Hour* (also available in a Plume edition), *The Dining Room, Scenes from American Life,* and *The Middle Ages.* He is also the author of three novels and the recipient of the Drama Desk Award and the Award of Merit from the Academy and Institute of Arts and Letters.

P9-EGN-489

OTHER PLAYS BY A. R. GURNEY

Scenes from American Life
Children
Richard Cory
The Wayside Motor Inn
The Middle Ages
The Dining Room
The Perfect Party
Sweet Sue
Another Antigone
The Cocktail Hour

Love Letters

and Two Other Plays:
The Golden Age
and
What I Did Last Summer

by

A. R. Gurney

With an Introduction by the Playwright

A PLUME BOOK

PLUME
Published by the Penguin Group
Penguin Books USA Inc., 375 Hudson Street, New York, New York 10014, U.S.A.
Penguin Books Ltd, 27 Wrights Lane, London W8 5TZ, England
Penguin Books Australia Ltd, Ringwood, Victoria, Australia
Penguin Books Canada Ltd, 2801 John Street, Markham, Ontario, Canada L3R 1B4
Penguin Books (N.Z.) Ltd, 182–190 Wairau Road, Auckland 10, New Zealand

Penguin Books Ltd, Registered Offices: Harmondsworth, Middlesex, England

First published by Plume, an imprint of New American Library,
a division of Penguin Books USA Inc.

First Printing, September, 1990
20   19

SOUND EFFECTS RECORD

The following sound effects record, which may be used in connection with production of this play, can be obtained from Thomas J. Valentino, Inc., 151 West 46th Street, New York, N.Y. 10036.

No. 5025—Door bell

SPECIAL NOTE ON SONGS AND RECORDINGS

For performance of such songs and recordings mentioned in this play as are in copyright, the permission of the copyright owners must be obtained; or other songs and recordings in the public domain substituted.

SPECIAL NOTE ON SONGS AND RECORDINGS

For performance of such songs and recordings mentioned in this play as are in copyright, the permission of the copyright owners must be obtained; or other songs and recordings in the public domain substituted.

(The following page constitutes an extension of this copyright page.)

SPECIAL NOTE

LIBRARY OF CONGRESS CATALOGING IN PUBLICATION DATA

Gurney, A. R. (Albert Ramsdell), 1930–
    Love letters, and two other plays : The golden age and What I did last summer / A.R. Gurney.
        p.   cm.
    ISBN 0-452-26501-0
    I. Title.
PS3557.U82L68   1990
812'.54—dc20   90-34177
                                                                                          CIP

Printed in the United States of America
Set in Bembo
Designed by Julian Hamer

PUBLISHER'S NOTE

INTRODUCTION

These are three plays about writing. They're also about other things, but writing would seem to strike a common chord between them. This might make them sound boring, and I hope they're not. Actually, writing can be a more active and exciting enterprise than most people think. Most writers like to take risks, and there's something thrilling about being out on a limb in your work and sensing that it might pay off. Writing is also fraught with dangers. You can easily go bonkers from the solitary confinement it seems to require. You can easily turn into an alcoholic from your frantic attempts to catch up with the world when you come up for air. And of course, if your writing is published or produced, there is the danger of having to run the gauntlet of critics, all practiced in inflicting subtle forms of cruel and unusual punishment.

Yet dangerous as it is, writing can be a kind of salvation for certain people. It's a way of making things manageable, by organizing them and putting them down in words. That's the case with Andy Ladd in *Love Letters*. He even says as much in his long letter to Melissa toward the end of Act One. Writing enables him to express feelings he never could articulate otherwise, and to make shape and order out of a world that seems vastly removed from the cozy, protected enclave in which he grew up. Writing to him is the only way out of the restrictive prison of the self, and the only way to extend himself toward the woman he loves.

Melissa, on the other hand, senses the problems inherent in writing. She knows instinctively that you can use words to hide as well as to reveal, and that letters can be ways of avoiding contact rather than of reaching out. She struggles mightily most of her life against Andy's attempts to induce her to play by his rules, and does what she can to respond in her own voice, on her own terms, through her drawings, through the telephone, and through constantly debunking his writing style. Writing is what brings Andy and Melissa together, but it is also what keeps them apart. Finally, Melissa is destroyed by a relationship that in a sense has become too dependent on the mail and the male. Andy, on the other hand, continues, even after her death, to find relief and comfort in writing letters, and can at least imagine her love and forgiveness as he writes to her mother at the end.

Love Letters, incidentally, began as a series of finger exercises as I was teaching myself how to use a computer. These began to cluster around a story, and once that took shape, and once I had committed myself to the form, I found it easy to write. I wasn't at all sure it was stageworthy, however, until I had a chance to read it with the actress Holland Taylor to a gathering at the New York Public Library, where I could sense the audience response. From then on, it quickly found a life for itself and engaged the interest of many fine actors.

Tom—"Peeping Tom"—in *The Golden Age* is in love with writing, or at least the idea of writing, as embodied in the works of Fitzgerald. Unlike Andy, who writes his way into a relationship with a woman, Tom tends to live vicariously through the writings of others. He teaches and writes about literature, and in his obsession with his idol, has tracked down the reclusive and mysterious Isabel Hastings Hoyt, who knew Fitzgerald and who may even possess a highly explicit, discarded chapter of *The Great Gatsby*. Isabel, on the other hand, has known enough writers not to romanticize them. Indeed, she seems to have been inordinately fond of even a *bad* writer, Walter Babcock McCoy. Nowadays, of course, she is concerned primarily with money, so that she can ensure the future of her beloved granddaughter, Virginia.

The duel between the wily old lady and the avid young professor is on one level a contest between someone who insists on personal privacy and someone who maintains that good writing is ultimately a public act. Beyond that, though, it is a conflict between a woman who believes in life and a man who yearns to retreat into the pages of a book. Being able to read Fitzgerald's purported description of what happened in bed between Daisy and Gatsby becomes more exciting to Tom than his own affair with Virginia. In the end, just as in *Love Letters*, boy loses girl because of his obsession with words on a page, though Virginia, unlike Melissa, seems to benefit from and survive the encounter.

The Golden Age, of course, is supposed to be a comic and contemporary version of Henry James's dark novella *The Aspern Papers*. I guess in writing it I was trying to work with some parallel between my own attempt to "steal" James's ingenious plot and Tom's attempt to steal Isabel's manuscript. James himself, it could be argued, took the plot, in part, from Pushkin's *Queen of Spades*, who in turn borrowed many of his elements from old tales about eager young men and mysterious secret-guarding crones. Even Chaucer's Wife of Bath's Tale contains some parallels. Writers like to take each other on across the centuries, but the limited success that *The Golden Age* has had in the theater makes me wonder whether, in this play, with Henry James leaning over my shoulder, I took on too big a man.

In any case, *The Golden Age* never seemed to kick into gear the way I hoped it would. It went through the usual number of initial readings, workshops, and even a try-out production at the Greenwich Theatre in London, but I never quite got it right. When we came into New York after a stint at the Kennedy Center, despite first-rate performances by Irene Worth, Stockard Channing, and Jeff Daniels, we lasted only a few weeks. I think now that in writing it, I fell into some of the same traps that its hero Tom falls into, becoming too obsessed with literary antecedents at the expense of what should have been happening right there on the stage.

If Tom is brought down from his excessive yearning for the world of literature by a tough-minded old woman, Charlie Higgins, in *What I Did Last Summer*, is initiated into the solaces of art by a somewhat similar mentor. Anna Trumbull, like Isabel Hastings Hoyt, is a woman "with a past," independent and reclusive and bemused by the world of respectability she has left behind. As she struggles to help Charlie find his "potential," she plants the seeds of a creative impulse that will ultimately grow into the very play we're experiencing. By the time the play is over, I would hope we had the sense that Charlie, through the process of writing this work, is finally managing to build a bridge between the two worlds that have almost torn him apart: the world of genteel respectability, represented by his mother, and that of a more open-minded bohemianism as shown by Anna.

I tried to make *What I did Last Summer* echo the old plots that were once popular in early Puritan literature: the Captivity Story, where a child is stolen from the community by Indians, initiated into a different way of life, and finally returned to "civilization," which absorbs and benefits from his more "natural" habits. This structure enabled me to dramatize the tension between the "stockade" life of duty and obligation and Anna's life of freedom and self-expression—a tension that seems to pervade *Love Letters* and *The Golden Age* as well.

The stage history of *What I Did Last Summer* is complicated. It was first done in a fairly successful summer tour, but it had its problems once it came into New York. Produced by the Circle Repertory Company, the production hit a series of snags and disagreements in rehearsal, with the result that we opened without either a director or the original lead. The critics didn't let us get away with it. Since then, though, the play has had considerable life in regional, community, and college theaters.

In any case, all three plays have to do with men who use writing as a mode of self-liberation, and their relationships with women who seem to be able to embrace a freer, more spirited life on their own. Writing, in some sense, is a way of mastering and shaping things, and in these plays we see women destroyed by the male obsession with dominance and control: Melissa finally retreats from Andy into depression and despair; Isabel dies attempting to protect her privacy from Tom; and Anna is exiled into oblivion once she gives in to Charlie's obsession with driving a car.

Furthermore, one could say that these are three plays about amateurs—lovers of writing who refuse to make a more total commitment that might be personally dangerous. Andy turns away from his affair with Melissa to settle for domestic ease and political respectability; Tom, in his obsession with another man's writing, loses Virginia; and Charlie, after years of dabbling with various forms of self-expression, finally finds his way into playwriting. Whether he'll stick with it, or be any good at it, we don't know.

A.R.G.

Love Letters

Love Letters was initially presented by the Long Wharf Theater (Arvin Brown, artistic director; M. Edgar Rosenblum, executive director) in New Haven, Connecticut, on November 3, 1988. It was directed by John Tillinger; the lighting was by Judy Rasmuson; and the production stage manager was Beverly J. Andreozzi. The cast was as follows:

ANDREW MAKEPEACE LADD III .John Rubinstein
MELISSA GARDNER . . . . .Joanna Gleason

Love Letters was subsequently presented by Roger L. Stevens, Thomas Viertel, Steven Baruch, and Richard Frankel at the Promenade Theatre (under the direction of Ben Sprecher and William P. Miller) in New York City on February 13, 1989. It was directed by John Tillinger; the lighting was by Dennis Parichy; casting was by Linda Wright; and the production stage manager was William H. Lang. The cast was as follows:

ANDREW MAKEPEACE LADD III .John Rubinstein
MELISSA GARDNER . . . . .Kathleen Turner

Love Letters opened on Broadway at the Edison Theatre on October 31, 1989. The cast was as follows:

ANDREW MAKEPEACE LADD III .Jason Robards
MELISSA GARDNER . . . . .Colleen Dewhurst

The following other actors have performed it in New York:

Richard Backus	Richard Kiley
Barbara Barrie	Swoosie Kurtz
Polly Bergen	Christine Lahti
Philip Bosco	Nancy Marchand
Stockard Channing	Marsha Mason
John Clark	Elizabeth McGovern
Stephen Collins	Elizabeth Montgomery
John Cunningham	Debra Mooney
Jane Curtin	James Naughton
Blythe Danner	Kate Nelligan
Bruce Davison	Rochelle Oliver
David Dukes	Remak Ramsay
Patricia Elliott	Lynn Redgrave
Robert Foxworth	Pamela Reed
Victor Garber	Christopher Reeve
George Grizzard	George Segal
A. R. Gurney	Josef Sommer
Julie Harris	Paul Sparer
Anthony Heald	Frances Sternhagen
John Heard	Elaine Stritch
George Hearn	Holland Taylor
Edward Herrmann	Richard Thomas
MaryBeth Hurt	Maria Tucci
William Hurt	Joan Van Ark
Timothy Hutton	Robert Vaughn
Dana Ivey	Christopher Walken
Judith Ivey	Fritz Weaver
E. Katherine Kerr	Treat Williams

Author's Note

This is a play, or rather a sort of a play, which needs no theater, no lengthy rehearsal, no special set, no memorization of lines, and no commitment from its two actors beyond the night of performance. It is designed simply to be read aloud by an actor and an actress of roughly the same age, sitting side by side at a table, in front of a group of people of any size. The actor might wear a dark gray suit, the actress a simple, expensive-looking dress. In a more formal production, the table and chairs might be reasonably elegant English antiques, and the actors' area may be isolated against a dark background by bright, focused lights. In performance, the piece would seem to work best if the actors didn't look at each other until the end, when Melissa might watch Andy as he reads his final letter. They *listen* eagerly and actively to each other along the way, however, much as we might listen to an urgent voice on a one-way radio, coming from far, far away.

PART ONE

ANDY: Andrew Makepeace Ladd, the Third, accepts with pleasure the kind invitation of Mr. and Mrs. Gilbert Channing Gardner for a birthday party in honor of their daughter Melissa on April 19th, 1937, at half past three o'clock . . .

MELISSA: Dear Andy: Thank you for the birthday present. I have a lot of Oz books, but not *The Lost Princess of Oz*. What made you give me that one? Sincerely yours, Melissa.

ANDY: I'm answering your letter about the book. When you came into second grade with that stuck-up nurse, you looked like a lost princess.

MELISSA: I don't believe what you wrote. I think my mother told your mother to get that book. I like the pictures more than the words. Now let's stop writing letters.

* * *

ANDY: I will make my *l*'s taller than my *d*'s.

MELISSA: I will close up my *a*'s and *o*'s.

ANDY: I will try to make longer *p*'s. Pass it on.

MELISSA: You're funny.

* * *

ANDY: Will you be my valentine?

MELISSA: Were you the one who sent me a valentine saying "Will you be my valentine?"

ANDY: Yes I sent it.

MELISSA: Then I will be. Unless I have to kiss you.

* * *

ANDY: When it's warmer out, can I come over and swim in your pool?

MELISSA: No you can't. I have a new nurse named Miss Hawthorne who thinks you'll give me infantile paralysis.

ANDY: Will you help me go down and get the milk and cookies during recess?

MELISSA: I will if you don't ask me to marry you again.

BOTH: I will not write personal notes in class, I will not write personal notes in class, I will not . . .

* * *

ANDY: Merry Christmas and Happy New Year. Love, Andy Ladd.

MELISSA: I made this card myself. It's not Santa Claus. It's a kangaroo jumping over a glass of orange juice. Do you like it? I like YOU. Melissa.

ANDY: My mother says I have to apologize in writing. I apologize for sneaking into the girls' bath-house while you were changing into your bathing suit. Tell Miss Hawthorne I apologize to her, too.

MELISSA: Here is a picture I drew of you and me without our bathing suits on. Guess which one is you. Don't show this to ANYONE. I love you.

ANDY: Here is a picture of Miss Hawthorne without her bathing suit on.

MELISSA: You can't draw very well, can you?

* * *

ANDY: Thank you for sending me the cactus plant stuck in the little donkey. I've gotten lots of presents here in the hospital and I have to write thank-you notes for every one. I hate it here. My throat is sore all the time from where they cut out my tonsils. They give me lots of ice cream, but they also take my temperature the wrong way.

★ ★ ★

MELISSA: Merry Christmas and Happy New Year. Why did they send you to another school this year?

ANDY: Merry Christmas. They think I should be with all boys.

★ ★ ★

MELISSA: You made me promise to send you a postcard. This is it.

ANDY: You're supposed to write personal notes on the backs of postcards. For example, here are some questions to help you think of things to say. Do you like Lake Saranac? Is it fun visiting your grandmother? Are your parents really getting divorced? Can you swim out into the deep part of the lake, or does Miss Hawthorne make you stay in the shallow part where it's all roped off? Is there anybody there my age? I mean boys. Please write answers to all these questions.

MELISSA: No. No. Yes. Yes. No.

★ ★ ★

ANDY: Dear Melissa. Remember me? Andy Ladd? They've sent me to camp so I can be with all boys again. This is quiet hour so we have to write home, but I've already done that, so I'm writing you. There's a real Indian here named Iron Crow who takes us on Nature walks and teaches us six new plants a day. This is O.K., except he forgot about poison ivy. I won the backstroke, which gives me two and a half gold stars. If I get over fifty gold stars by Parent's Day, then I win a Leadership Prize which is what my father expects of me. I'm making a napkin-ring in shop which is worth four stars and which is either for my mother or for you. I hope you'll write me back, because when the mail comes every morning, they shout out our names and it would be neat to walk up and get a letter from a girl.

MELISSA: Help! Eeeek! Yipes! I can't write LETTERS! It took me HOURS just to write "Dear Andy." I wrote my father because I miss him so much, but to write a BOY! Hell's Bells and Oriental Smells! I'm sending you this picture I drew of our cat instead. Don't you love his expression? It's not quite right, but I tried three times. I drew those jiggly lines around his tail because sometimes the tail behaves like a completely separate person. I love that tail. There's a part of me that feels like the tail. Oh, and here's some bad news. My mother's gotten married again to a man named Hooper McPhail. HELP! LEMME OUTA HERE!

ANDY: I liked the cat. Is that the cat you threw in the pool that time when we were playing over at your house in third grade?

MELISSA: No, that was a different cat entirely.

★   ★   ★

ANDY: This is a dumb Halloween card and wouldn't scare anyone, but I'm really writing about dancing school. My parents say I have to go this year, but I don't see why I have to. I can't figure out why they keep sending us away from girls and then telling us we have to be with them. Are you going to dancing school also? Just write Yes or No, since you hate writing.

MELISSA: Yes.

★ ★ ★

ANDY: Dear Mrs. McPhail. I want to apologize to you for my behavior in the back of your car coming home last night from dancing school. Charlie and I were just goofing around and I guess it just got out of hand. I'm sorry you had to pull over to the curb and I'm sorry we tore Melissa's dress. My father says you should send me the bill and I'll pay for it out of my allowance.

MELISSA: Dear Andy. Mummy brought your letter up here to Lake Placid. She thought it was cute. I thought it was dumb. I could tell your father made you write it. You and I both know that the fight in the car was really Charlie's fault. And Charlie never apologized, thank God. That's why I like him, actually. As for you, you shouldn't always do what your parents WANT, Andy. Even at dancing school you're always doing just the RIGHT THING all the time. You're a victim of your parents sometimes. That was why I picked Charlie to do the rumba with me that time. He at least hacks around occasionally. I'm enclosing a picture I drew of a dancing bear on a chain. That's you, Andy. Sometimes. I swear.

ANDY: I know it seems jerky, but I like writing, actually. I like writing compositions in English, I like writing letters, I like writing you. I wanted to write that letter to your mother because I knew you'd see it, so it was like talking to you when you weren't here. And when you couldn't *interrupt*. (Hint, hint.) My father says everyone should write letters as much as they can. It's a dying art. He says letters are a way of presenting yourself in the best possible light to another person. I think that, too.

MELISSA: I think you sound too much like your father. But I'm not going to argue by MAIL and anyway the skiing's too good.

ANDY: Get well soon. I'm sorry you broke your leg.

MELISSA: Mummy says I broke it purposely because I'm a self-destructive person and went down Whiteface Mountain without asking permission. All I know is I wish I had broken my arm instead so I'd have a good excuse not to write LETTERS. I'm enclosing a picture I drew of the bed pan. I'm SERIOUS! Don't you love its shape?

★   ★   ★

ANDY: Andrew M. Ladd, III, accepts with pleasure the kind invitation of Mrs. R. Ferguson Brown for a dinner in honor of her granddaughter Melissa Gardner before the Children's Charity Ball.

MELISSA: I'm writing this letter because I'm scared if I called you up, I'd start crying, right on the telephone. I'm really MAD at you, Andy. Don't you know that when you're invited to a dinner before a dance, you're supposed to dance with the person giving it at least TWICE. And I don't mean my grandmother either. That's why they *give* dinner parties. So people get *danced* with. I notice you danced with Ginny Waters, but you never danced with me once. I just think it's rude, that's all. Straighten up and fly right, Andy. How do you expect to get anywhere in life if you're rude to women? Nuts to you, Andy, and that goes double on Sunday!

ANDY: I didn't dance with you because I've got a stretched groin. If you don't know what that means, look it up some time. I was going to tell you in person but I got embarrassed. I stretched it playing hockey last week. The only reason I danced with Ginny Waters is she takes tiny steps, but you always make me do those big spins and we could have gotten into serious trouble. I tried it out at home with my mother first, and it hurt like hell. That's why I didn't dance with you. I'm using a heating pad now and maybe we can dance next week at the junior assemblies.

MELISSA: I don't believe that hockey stuff. I think Ginny Waters stretched your groin. And next time you cut in, I'm going to stretch the other one.

ANDY: Huh? You obviously don't know what a groin is.

MELISSA: You obviously don't know what a joke is.

* * *

MELISSA: Merry Christmas and Happy New Year. Guess what? I'm going to a psychiatrist now. My mother says it will do me a world of good. Don't tell anyone, though. It's supposed to be a big secret.

ANDY: Merry Christmas and Happy New Year. I have a question and would you please write the answer *by mail*, because sometimes when you call, my mother listens on the telephone, and when she doesn't my little brother does. Here's the question: do you talk about sex with the psychiatrist?

MELISSA: I talk about sex all the time. It's terribly expensive, but I think it's worth it.

ANDY: If I went to a psychiatrist, I'd talk about you. Seriously. I would. I think about you quite often.

MELISSA: Sometimes I think you just like me because I'm richer than you are. Sometimes I really have that feeling. I think you like the pool, and the elevator in my grandmother's house, and Simpson in his butler's coat coming in with ginger ale and cookies on a silver tray. I think you like all that stuff just as much as you like me.

ANDY: All I know is my mother keeps saying you'd make a good match. She says if I ever married you, I'd be set up for life. But I think it's really just physical attraction. That's why I liked going into the elevator with you at your grandmother's that time. Want to try it again?

* * *

MELISSA: HELP! LEMME OUTA HERE! They shipped
me off to this nunnery! It's the end of the absolute
WORLD! We have to wear these sappy middy-blouses,
and learn POSTURE in gym, and speak French out LOUD
in class. "Aide-moi, mon chevalier!" Oh God, it's crappy
here. All the girls squeal and shriek, and you can hear
them barfing in the bathroom after the evening meal. We
can only go to Hartford one day a week IF we find a
chaperone, and there are only two dances with boys a
year, and if we're caught drinking, even *beer*, it's wham,
bam, onto the next train and home, which is WORSE!
Can you come visit me some Sunday afternoon? We can
invite boys to tea from four to six. There are all these
biddies sitting around keeping watch, but if the weather's
good, we could walk up and down the driveway before
we have to sign in for evening prayers. They've made me
room with this fat, spoiled Cuban bitch who has nine pairs
of shoes, and all she does is lie on her bed and listen to
Finian's Rainbow. "How are Things in Glocca Morra?"
Who gives a shit how things are *there*? It's here where
they're miserable. The walls of this cell are puke-green,
and you can't pin anything up except school banners and
pictures of your stupid family. What family? Am I supposed to sit and look at a picture of Hooper McPhail?
Come save me, Andy. Or at least WRITE! Just so I hear a
boy's voice, even on paper.

ANDY: Just got your letter. They shipped me off too. Last-
minute decision. Your mother told my mother it would
do me good. She said I was a diamond in the rough. I'll
write as soon as I'm smoother.

MELISSA: Dear Diamond. You, too? Oh, I give up. Why do
they keep pushing us together and then pulling us apart? I
think we're all being brought up by a bunch of foolish

farts. Now we'll *have* to write letters which I hate. But don't let them smooth you out, Andy. I like the rough parts. In fact, sometimes I think you ought to be a little rougher. Love. Me.

ANDY: I'm very sorry to be so late in replying but I haven't had much time. I also have a lot of obligations. I have to write my parents once a week, and three out of four grandparents, *separately*, once a month, and Minnie, our cook, who sent me a box of fudge. Plus I have all my schoolwork to do, including a composition once a week for English and another for history. My grandmother gave me a new Parker 51 and some writing paper with my name on it as a going-away present, but still, that's a lot of writing I have to do. Last week I was so tied up I skipped my weekly letter to my parents, and my father called the school long-distance about it. I had to go up on the carpet in front of the Rector and say I wasn't sick or anything, I was just working, and so I had to write my parents three pages to make up for the week I missed. So that's why I haven't written till now. (Whew!) School is going well, I guess. In English, we're now finishing up Milton's *Paradise Lost*. In history, we're studying the causes and results of the Thirty Years War. I think the Catholics caused it. In Latin, we're translating Cicero's orations against Catiline. "How long, O Catiline, will you abuse our patience?" When I get home, I'm going to try that on my little brother. In French, we have to sit and listen to Mr. Thatcher read out loud all the parts in *Andromache*, by Jean Racine. It's supposed to be a great masterpiece, but the class comes right after football practice, so it's a little hard to stay awake. In Sacred Studies, we have to compare and contrast all four gospels. It's hard to believe they're all talking about the same guy. In Math, we're trying to factor with two unknowns. Sometimes I let X be me and Y be you, and you'd be amazed how it comes out.

My grades are pretty good. They post your weekly average outside study hall and last week I got 91.7 overall average. Not bad, eh? I got a letter from my grandfather telling me not to be first in my class because only the Jews are first. I wrote him and told him I wasn't first, but even if I was, there are no Jews here. We have a few Catholics, but they're not too smart, actually. I don't think you can be smart and Catholic at the same time.

I was elected to the Student Council and I'm arguing for three things: one, I think we should have outside sports, rather than keeping them all intramural. I think it would be better to play with Exeter than just play with ourselves. Two, I think we should have more than one dance a year. I think female companionship can be healthy occasionally, even for younger boys. And three, I think we should only have to go to chapel *once* on Sunday. I think it's important to pray to be a better guy, and all that, but if you have to do it all day long, you can get quite boring. And if you get boring to yourself, think how boring you must be to God.

I'm playing left tackle on the third team, and I'll be playing hockey, *of course*, this winter, and I think I'll try rowing this spring since I always stank at baseball.

Now I have to memorize the last five lines of *Paradise Lost*. Hold it . . . Back in a little while . . . There. That wasn't so hard, maybe because it reminds me of you and me, sent away from home. I'll write it down for you:
Some natural tears they'd dropp'd, but wip'd them soon;
The World was all before them, where to choose
Their place of rest, and providence their guide:
They hand in hand with wand'ring steps and slow,
Through Eden took their solitary way.
There you are. I wrote that without looking at the book, and it's right, too, because I just checked it, word by word. It's not so bad, is it? In fact, it sounds great if you

recite it in the bathroom, when no one is in the shower or taking a dump. Love, Andy.

MELISSA: Thanks for your letter which was a little too long. I guess you have a lot of interesting things to say, Andy, but some of them are not terribly interesting to me. I want to hear more about your FEELINGS. For instance, here are MY feelings. This place STINKS, but I don't want to go back home because Hooper McPhail stinks, and I haven't heard of another boarding school that DOESN'T stink, which means that LIFE stinks in general. Those are my feelings for this week. Write soon. Love, me.

ANDY: One feeling I have almost all the time is that I miss my dog, Porgy. Remember him? Our black cocker who peed in the vestibule when you patted him when you came back to our house after the skating party. I miss him all the time. Some of the masters up here have dogs, and when I pat them I miss Porgy even more. I dream about him. I wrote a composition about him for English called "Will He Remember?" and got a 96 on it. It was about how I remember him, but will he remember me? I have a picture of him on my bureau right next to my parents. By the way, could I have your picture, too?

MELISSA: Here's a picture of me taken at the Hartford bus station. I was all set to run away and then decided not to. This is all you get until I get my braces off Christmas vacation. Don't look at my hair. I'm changing it. By the way, do you know a boy there named Spencer Willis? There's a girl here, Annie Abbott, who met him in Edgartown last summer and thinks he's cute. Would you ask him what he thinks of her?

ANDY: Spencer Willis says Annie Abbott is a potential nympho. I'm sorry to tell you this, but it's true.

MELISSA: Annie says to tell Spencer he's a total turkey. Tell him she'd write and say so herself but she's scared of barfing all over the page.

ANDY: Do you get out for Thanksgiving? We don't, because of the war.

MELISSA: We do, but I don't. I've been grounded just for smoking one lousy Chesterfield out behind the art studio. So now I have to stay here and eat stale turkey with Cubans and Californians. That's all right. I was supposed to meet Mummy in New York, but it looks like she can't be there anyway because she's going to Reno to divorce Hooper McPhail. Yippee! Yay! He was a jerk and a pill, and he used to bother me in bed, if you must know.

★ ★ ★

ANDY: I liked seeing you Christmas vacation, particularly with your braces off. I really liked necking with you in the Watsons' rumpus room. Will you go steady with me?

MELISSA: I don't believe in going steady. It's against my religion. I hated that stuff with all those pairs of pimply people in the Watsons' basement, leaning on each other, swaying to that dumb music with all the lights off. If that's going steady, I say screw it. My mother says you should meet as many boys as you can before you have to settle down and marry one of them. That way you'll make less of a mistake. It didn't work for her but maybe it will work for me.

ANDY: Can we at least go to the movies together during spring vacation?

MELISSA: I don't know, Andy. I like seeing you, but I don't want to go home much any more. My mother gets drunk a lot, if you must know, and comes into my room all the time, and talks endlessly about I don't know what because she slurs her words. The only really good time I had was when I came over to your house Christmas Eve. That was fun. Singing around the piano, hanging up the stockings, playing Chinese Checkers with your brother, helping your mother with the gravy. I liked all that. You may not have as much money as we have, but you've got a better family. So spring vacation I'm going to visit my grandmother in Palm Beach. Ho hum. At least I'll get a tan. P.S. Enclosed is a picture I drew of your dog Porgy who I remember from Christmas Eve. The nose is wrong, but don't you think the eyes are good?

ANDY: I'm stroking the 4th crew now. Yesterday, I rowed number 2 on the 3rd. Tomorrow I may row number 6 on the 2nd or number 4 on the 5th. Who knows? You get out there and work your butt off, and the launch comes alongside and looks you over, and the next day they post a list on the bulletin board saying who will row what. They never tell you what you did right or wrong, whether you're shooting your slide or bending your back or what. They just post the latest results for all to see. Some days I think I'm doing really well, and I get sent down two crews. One day I was obviously hacking around, and they moved me UP. There's no rhyme or reason. I went to Mr. Clark who is the head of rowing and I said, "Look, Mr. Clark. There's something wrong about this system. People are constantly moving up and down and no one knows why. It doesn't seem to have anything to do with whether you're good or bad, strong or weak, coordinated or uncoordinated. It all seems random, *sir*." And Mr. Clark said "That's life, Andy." And walked away. Well maybe that's life, but it doesn't *have* to be life. You could easily make rules which made sense, so the good ones moved up and the bad ones moved down, and people *knew* what was going on. I'm serious. I'm thinking about going to law school later on.

MELISSA: Your last letter was too much about rowing. Do you know a boy there named Steve Scully? I met him down in Florida, and he said he went to your school, and was on the first crew. He said he was the fastest rower in the boat. Is that true, or was he lying? I think he may have been lying.

ANDY: Steve Scully was lying. He doesn't even row. And if he did, and rowed faster than everyone else in the same boat, he'd mess the whole thing up. He said he got to second base with you. Is that true?

MELISSA: Steve Scully is a lying son of a bitch, and you can tell him I said so.

★   ★   ★

ANDY: Will you be around this summer? I think I've got a summer job caddying, so no more camp, thank God.

MELISSA: I'll be visiting my father in California. I haven't seen him in four years. He has a new wife, and I have two half-sisters now. It's like going to find a whole new family. Oh I hope, I hope . . .

ANDY: Do you like California?

★   ★   ★

Write me about California. How's your second family?

★   ★   ★

Did you get my letters? I checked with your mother, and I had the correct address. How come you haven't answered me all summer?

★   ★   ★

Back at school now. Hope everything's O.K. with you. Did you get my letters out in California, or did you have a wicked stepmother who confiscated them?

MELISSA: I don't want to talk about California. Ever. For a while I thought I had two families, but now I know I really don't have any. You're very lucky, Andy. You don't know it, but you are. But maybe I'm lucky, too. In another way. I was talking to Mrs. Wadsworth who comes in from Hartford to teach us art. She says I have a real talent both in drawing and in painting, and she's going to try me out in pottery as well. She says some afternoon she's going to take me just by myself to her studio in Hartford, and we'll do life drawings of her lover in just a jock-strap! Don't laugh. She says art and sex are sort of the same thing.

★　★　★

ANDY: Dear Melissa. I have four questions, so please concentrate. One: will you come up to the mid-winter dance? Two, If so, can you arrive on the eleven-twenty-two Friday night train? Three, Does the Rector's wife have to write your Headmistress telling her where you will be staying? Four. Does the Rector's wife also have to write your mother?

MELISSA: The answer is yes, except for my mother, who won't care.

★　★　★

ANDY: I have to tell you this, right off the bat. I'm really goddam mad at you. I invite you up here for the only dance my class has been able to go to since we got here, I meet you at the train and buy you a vanilla milkshake and bring you out to school in a taxi, I score two goals for you during the hockey game the next afternoon, I buy you the eight-dollar gardenia corsage, I make sure your dance card is filled with the most regular guys in the school, and then what happens? I now hear that you sneaked off with Bob Bartram during the Vienna Waltz, and necked with him in the coatroom. I heard that from two guys! And then Bob himself brought it up yesterday at breakfast. He says he French-kissed you and touched BOTH your breasts. I tried to punch him but Mr. Enbody restrained me. I'm really sore, Melissa. I consider this a betrayal of everything I hold near and dear. Particularly since you would hardly even let me kiss you good night after we had cocoa at the Rector's. And you know what I'm talking about, too! So don't expect any more letters from me, or any telephone calls either during spring vacation. Sincerely yours.

MELISSA: Sorry, sorry, sorry. I AM! I HATE that Bob Bartram. I hated him even when I necked with him. I know you won't believe that, but it's true. You can be attracted to someone you hate. Well, maybe *you* can't, but I can. So all right, I necked with him, but he never touched my chest, and if he says he did, he should be strung up by his testicles. You tell him that, for me, at breakfast! Anyway, I got carried away, Andy, and I'm a stupid bitch, and I'm sorry. I felt so guilty about it that I didn't want to kiss you after the cocoa.

And besides, Andy. Gulp. Er. Ah. Um. How do I say this? With you it's different. You're like a friend to me. You're like a brother. I've never had a brother, and I don't have too many friends, so you're both, Andy. You're it. My mother says you must never say that to a man, but I'm saying it anyway and it's true. Maybe if I didn't know you so well, maybe if I hadn't grown up with you, maybe if we hadn't written all these goddamn LETTERS all the time, I could have kissed you the way I kissed Bob Bartram.

Oh, but PLEASE let's see each other spring vacation. Please. I count on you, Andy. I NEED you. I think sometimes I'd go stark raving mad if I didn't have you to hold onto. I really think that sometimes. Much love.

★ ★ ★

Happy Easter! I know no one sends Easter cards except maids, but here's mine anyway, drawn with my own hot little hands. I drew those tears on that corny bunny on the left because it misses you so much, but maybe I've just made it all the cornier.

★ ★ ★

Greetings from Palm Beach. Decided to visit my grandmother. Yawn, yawn. I'm a whiz at backgammon and gin-rummy. Hear you took Gretchen Lascelles to see *Quo Vadis* and sat in the *loges* and put your arm around her and smoked! Naughty, naughty!

★ ★ ★

Back at school, but not for long, that's for sure. Caught nipping gin in the woods with Bubbles Harriman. Have to pack my trunk by tonight and be out tomorrow. Mummy's frantically pulling strings all over the Eastern Seaboard for another school. Mrs. Wadsworth, my art teacher, thinks I should chuck it all and go to Italy and study art. What do you think? Oh, please write, Andy, PLEASE. I need your advice, or are you too busy thinking about Gretchen Lascelles?

★ ★ ★

ANDY: To answer your question about Italy, I think you're too young to go. My mother said she had a roommate once who went to Italy in the summer, and the Italians pinched her all the time on the rear end. Mother says she became thoroughly overstimulated. So I think you should go to another school, graduate, go to college, and maybe after that, when you're more *mature*, you could go to Italy. That's my advice, for what it's worth, which is probably not much, the way things are going between you and me.

★ ★ ★

MELISSA: Here I am at Emma Willard's Academy for Young Lesbians. Help! Lemme outa here! "Plus ça change, plus c'est le same shit." Are you coming straight home this June because I am. I want to see you. Or are you still in love with Gretchen Lascelles?

ANDY: For your information, I am not taking Gretchen Lascelles out any more. I brought her home after the Penneys' party, and my father caught us on the couch. He told me that he didn't care what kind of girls I took out, as long as I didn't bring them around my mother. Even though my mother was up in bed. Still, I guess Gretchen can be embarrassing to older people.

MELISSA: I hope to see you in June, then.

ANDY: Can't come home in June. Sorry. I have to go and be a counselor at the school camp for poor kids from the urban slums. I'm vice-president of my class now, and I'm supposed to set an example of social responsibility all through July. I'll be writing you letters, though, and I hope you'll write me.

MELISSA: I don't want to write letters all the time. I really don't. I want to see you.

ANDY: You just need more confidence in your letter-writing ability. Sometimes you manage to attain a very vivid style.

MELISSA: Won't you please just stop writing about writing, and come home and go to the Campbells' sports party before you go up to that stupid camp? PLEASE! I behave better when you're around. In PERSON! PLEASE!

* * *

ANDY: Greetings from New Hampshire. This card shows the town we're near, where we sneak in and buy beer. We're cleaning the place up now, and putting out the boat docks, and caulking the canoes, because the kids arrive tomorrow. Gotta go. Write soon.

MELISSA: I miss you. I really wish you had come to the Campbells' sports party.

ANDY: Dear Melissa. Sandy McCarthy arrived from home for the second shift here at camp, and he told me all about the Campbells' sports party. He said you wore a two-piece bathing suit and ran around goosing girls and pushing boys into the pool. Do you enjoy that sort of crap? He said the other girls were furious at you. Don't you want the respect of other women? Sandy also said you let Bucky Zeller put a tennis ball into your cleavage. Are you a nympho or what? Don't you ever like just sitting down somewhere and making conversation? Sandy says you're turning into a hot box. Do you like having that reputation? Hell, I thought there was a difference between you and Gretchen Lascelles. Maybe I was wrong. Don't you care about anything in this world except hacking around? Don't you feel any obligation to help the poor people, for example? Sometimes I think your big problem is you're so rich you don't have enough to do, and so you start playing grab-ass with people. I'm sorry to say these things, but what Sandy told me made me slightly disgusted, frankly.

* * *

I wrote you a letter from New Hampshire. Did you receive it?

* * *

Are you there, or are you visiting your grandmother, or what?

* * *

Are you sore at me? I'll bet you're sore at me.

* * *

I'm sorry. I apologize. I'm a stuffy bastard sometimes, aren't I?

* * *

The hell with you, then.

MELISSA: Oooh. Big, tough Andy using four-letter words like hell.
ANDY: Screw you!
MELISSA: Don't you wish you could!
ANDY: Everyone else seems to be.
MELISSA: Don't believe everything you read in the papers.

* * *

Dear Andrew Makepeace Ladd, the Turd: I just want you to know you hurt me very much. I just want you to know that. Now let's just leave each other ALONE for a while. All right? All right.

* * *

ANDY: Dear Melissa: My mother wrote me that your grandmother had died. Please accept my deepest sympathies.

MELISSA: Thank you for your note about my grandmother. I loved her a lot even though she could be a little boring.

ANDY: Congratulations on getting into Briarcliff. I hear it's great.

MELISSA: Thank you for your note about Briarcliff. It's not great and you know it. In fact, it's a total pit. But it's close to New York and I can take the train in and take drawing at the Institute three days a week. And in two years, if I stick it out, Mummy's promised that I can go live in Florence. I hope you like Yale.

ANDY: Would you consider coming to the Yale-Dartmouth game, Saturday, Oct 28th?

MELISSA: I'll be there.

ANDY: Uh-oh. Damn! I'm sorry, Melissa. I have to cancel. My parents have decided to visit that weekend, and they come first, according to them. My mother says she'd love to have you with us, but my father thinks you can be somewhat distracting.

MELISSA: You and your parents. Let me know when you decide to grow up.

ANDY: How about the Harvard game, November 16th?

MELISSA: Do you plan to grow up at the Harvard game?

ANDY: Give me a chance. I might surprise you.

MELISSA: O.K. Let's give it a try. You should know that I'm even richer now than when you said I was rich, thanks to poor Granny. I plan to drive up to the front gate of Calhoun College in my new red Chrysler convertible, and sit there stark naked, honking my horn and drinking champagne and flashing at all the freshmen.

ANDY: Here's the schedule. We'll have lunch at Calhoun around noon. Then drive out to the game. Then there's a Sea-Breeze party at the Fence Club afterwards, and an Egg Nog brunch at Saint Anthony's the next day. I'll

reserve a room for you at the Taft or the Duncan, probably the Taft, since the Duncan is a pretty seedy joint.

MELISSA: Make it the Duncan. I hear the Taft is loaded with
parents, all milling around the lobby, keeping tabs on
who goes up in the elevators. Can't WAIT till the 16th.

ANDY: The Duncan it is. Hubba hubba, Goodyear rubba!

★　★　★

MELISSA: Dear Andy. This is supposed to be a thank-you
note for the Yale-Harvard weekend, but I don't feel like
writing one, and I think you know why. Love, Melissa.

ANDY: Dear Melissa. I keep thinking about the weekend. I
can't get it out of my mind. It wasn't much good, was it?
I don't mean just the Duncan, I mean the whole thing. We
didn't really click, did we? I always had the sense that you
were looking over my shoulder, looking for someone
else, and ditto with me. Both of us seemed to be expect-
ing something different from what was there.

As for the Hotel Duncan, I don't know. Maybe I had
too many Sea-Breezes. Maybe you did. But what I really
think is that there were too many people in the hotel
room. Besides you and me, it seemed my mother was
there, egging us on, and my father, shaking his head, and
your mother zonked out on the couch, and Miss Hawthorne and your *grand*mother, sitting on the sidelines,
watching us like hawks. Anyway, I was a dud. I admit it.
I'm sorry. I went to the Infirmary on Monday and talked to
the doctor about it, and he said these things happen all the
time. Particularly when there's a lot of pressure involved.
The woman doesn't have to worry about it so much, but
the man does. Anyway, it didn't happen with Gretchen
Lascelles. You can write her and ask her if you want.

MELISSA: You know what I think is wrong? These letters.
These goddamn letters. That's what's wrong with us, in

my humble opinion. I know you more from your LET-TERS than I do in person. Maybe that's why I was looking over your shoulder. I was looking for the person who's been in these letters all these years. Or for the person who's NOT in these letters. I don't know. All I know is you're not quite the same when I see you, Andy. You're really not. I'm not saying you're a jerk in person. I'm not saying that at all. I'm just saying that all this letter-writing has messed us up. It's a bad habit. It's made us seem like people we're not. So maybe what was wrong was that there were two people *missing* in the Hotel Duncan that night: namely, the real you and the real me.

ANDY: Whatever the matter is, we're in real trouble, you and I. That I realize. So now, what do we do about it? Maybe we should just concentrate on dancing together. Then we can still hold each other and move together and get very subtly sexy with each other, and not have to deliver the goods all the time, if you know what I mean. Come to think of it, maybe that's why they sent us to dancing school in the first place. Maybe that's why dancing was invented.

MELISSA: At least we should stop writing LETTERS for a while. You could start telephoning me, actually. Here is our dorm number: WILSON 1-2486.

ANDY: I hate talking to you on the telephone. Yours is in the hall and ours is right by the college dining room. People are always coming and going and making cracks. Telephoning is not letter-writing at all.

MELISSA: I called the telephone company and they've put a private phone in my room. ROGERS 2-2403. It's sort of expensive, but at least we can TALK!

★ ★ ★

ANDY: The reason I'm writing is because your phone's always busy. Or else ours is. And I can't afford a private one. Maybe we should just start writing letters again.

MELISSA: No letters! Please! Now order that telephone! I'll lend you the dough. Just think about it. You can talk back and forth, and hear someone's real voice, and get to know someone in LIFE, rather than on WRITING PAPER, for God's sake! Now get that phone! Please!

★　★　★

ANDY: I'm writing because when I telephoned, you just hung up on me. One thing about letters: you can't hang up on them.

MELISSA: You can tear up letters, though. Enclosed are the pieces. Send them to Angela Atkinson at Sarah Lawrence.

ANDY: What the hell is the matter?

MELISSA: I hear you're now writing long letters twice a week to Angela Atkinson, that's what's the matter.

ANDY: O.K. Here goes. The reason I'm writing Angie Atkinson is because I just don't think I can stop writing letters, particularly to girls. As I told you before, in some ways I feel most alive when I'm holed up in some corner, writing things down. I pick up a pen, and almost immediately everything seems to take shape around me. I love to write. I love writing my parents because then I become the ideal son. I love writing essays for English, because then I am for a short while a true scholar. I love writing letters to the newspaper, notes to my friends, Christmas cards, anything where I have to put down words. I love writing you. You most of all. I always have. I feel like a true lover when I'm writing you. This letter, which I'm writing with my own hand, with my own pen, in my own penmanship, comes from me and no one else, and is a present of myself to you. It's not typewritten, though

I've learned how to type. There's no copy of it, though I suppose I could use a carbon. And it's not a telephone call, which is dead as soon as it is over. No, this is just me, me the way I write, the way my writing is, the way I want to be to you, giving myself to you across a distance, not keeping or retaining any part of it for myself, giving this piece of myself to you totally, and you can tear me up and throw me out, or keep me, and read me today, tomorrow, any time you want until you die.

MELISSA: Oh Boy, Andy. Love, Melissa.

ANDY: No, I meant what I wrote in my last letter. I've thought about it. I've thought about all those dumb things which were done to us when we were young. We had absent parents, slapping nurses, stupid rules, obsolete schooling, empty rituals, hopelessly confusing sexual customs . . . oh my God, when I think about it now, it's almost unbelievable, it's a fantasy, it's like back in the Oz books, the way we grew up. But they gave us an out in the Land of Oz. They made us write. They didn't make us write particularly well. And they didn't always give us important things to write about. But they did make us sit down, and organize our thoughts, and convey those thoughts on paper as clearly as we could to another person. Thank God for that. That saved us. Or at least saved me. So I have to keep writing letters. If I can't write them to you, I have to write them to someone else. I don't think I could ever stop writing completely. Now can I come up and see you next weekend, or better yet won't you please escape from that suburban Sing-Sing and come down here and see me? I wrote my way into this problem, and goddamn it, I'm writing my way out. I'll make another reservation at the Hotel Duncan and I promise I'll put down my pen and give you a better time.

MELISSA: Dear Andy: Guess what? Right while I was in the middle of reading your letter, Jack Duffield telephoned from Amherst and asked me for a weekend up there. So I said yes before I got to where you asked me. Sorry, sweetie, but it looks like the telephone wins in the end.

ANDY: Dear Melissa: Somehow I don't think this is the end. It could be, but I don't really think it is. At least I hope it isn't. Love, Andy.

END OF PART ONE

(The event works best if everyone takes a short break at this point.)

PART TWO

MELISSA: Hey! Yoo-hoo! Look where I am! Florence, Ooops, I mean Firenze! I LOVE it!

ANDY: What are you doing in Florence?

MELISSA: What am I doing? I'm painting, among other things.

ANDY: Good luck on the painting. Go slow on the other things.

★ ★ ★

ANDY: Merry Christmas.

MELISSA: Buon Natale . . .

ANDY: Happy Birthday . . . Mother wrote you won an art prize in Perugia. She said it was a big deal. Congratulations . . .

MELISSA: Congratulations on making Scroll and Key, whatever that is . . .

ANDY: Merry Christmas from the Land of Oz . . .

MELISSA: Felicita Natividad from the Costa del Sol . . .

ANDY: Happy Birthday from the Sterling Library . . .

MELISSA: Hear you graduated summa cum laude and with all sorts of prizes. Sounds disgusting . . .

ANDY: Anchors Aweigh! Here I am, looking like Henry Fonda in *Mister Roberts*, writing this during the midwatch on the bridge of a giant attack aircraft carrier, churning through the Mediterranean, in the wake of Odysseus and Lord Nelson and Richard Halliburton. You'll be pleased to know our guns are loaded, our planes in position, and our radar is constantly scanning the skies, all designed simply and solely to protect you against communism. The next time you see me, I want you to salute.

MELISSA: I should have known you'd join the Navy. Now you can once again be with all boys.

ANDY: We come into La Spezia in January. Could we meet?

MELISSA: Sorry. I'll be in Zermatt in January.

ANDY: Ship will be in Mediterranean all spring. We'll come into Naples, March 3, 4, or 5? How about standing on the pier and waving us in?

MELISSA: As the French say, "Je suis desolée." Am meeting Mother in Paris in March. Why don't you sail up the Seine?

ANDY: Merry Christmas from Manila. I've been transferred to an Admiral's staff . . .

MELISSA: Happy New Year from Aspen . . .

ANDY: What are you doing in Aspen?

MELISSA: Going steadily downhill.

ANDY: Hello from Hong Kong . . .

MELISSA: Goodbye to San Francisco . . .

ANDY: Konichiwa. Ohayo Gozaimas. Shore duty in Japan . . .

MELISSA: Hey, you! Rumor hath it you're hooked up with some little Jap bar-girl out there. Say it isn't so . . .

* * *

Mother wrote that you're living with some Japanese geisha girl and your family's all upset. Is that TRUE?

* * *

Did you get my letter? You're so far away, and your Navy address is so peculiar that I'm not sure I'm reaching you. I hear you're seriously involved with a lovely Japanese lady. Would you write me about her?

ANDY: Merry Christmas and Happy New Year. I thought you might appreciate this card. It's a print by the nineteenth-century artist Hiroshige. It's called "Two Lovers Meeting on a Bridge in the Rain." Love, Andy.

MELISSA: Hey, you sly dog! Are you getting subtle in your old age? Are you trying to TELL me something? If so, tell me MORE!

* * *

I told my psychiatrist about the great love affair you're having in Japan. I said I felt suddenly terribly jealous. He said that most American men have to get involved with a dark-skinned woman before they can connect with the gorgeous blonde goddesses they really love. He brought up James Fenimore Cooper and Faulkner and John Ford movies and went on and on. Is that TRUE? Write me what you think. I'm dying to hear from you.

* * *

Did you get my last letter? I hope I didn't sound flip. Actually I've just become involved with someone, too. His first name is Darwin and he works on Wall Street where he believes in the survival of the fittest. I'd love to hear from you.

* * *

Your mother told my mother that you've decided to marry your Japanese friend and bring her home. Oh no! Gasp, Sob, Sigh. Say it isn't so . . .

* * *

I've decided to marry Darwin. He doesn't know it yet, but he will. Won't you at least wish me luck?

★ ★ ★

ANDY: Lieutenant Junior Grade Andrew M. Ladd, III, regrets that he is unable to accept the kind invitation of . . .

MELISSA: Dear Andy. Thank you for the lovely Japanese bowl. I'll put flowers in it when you come to visit us. *If* you come to visit us. And *if* you bring flowers. Maybe you'll just bring your Japanese war bride, and we can all sit around and discuss *Rashomon*. I know you'll like Darwin. When he laughs, it's like Pinocchio turning into a donkey. We're living in a carriage house in New Canaan close to the train station, and I've got a studio all of my own. P.S. Won't you PLEASE write me about your big romance? Mother says your parents won't even talk about it any more.

ANDY: Dear Melissa: I'm writing to tell you this. Outside of you, and I *mean* outside of you, this was probably the most important thing that ever happened to me. And I mean *was*. Because it's over, it's gone, and I'm coming home, and that's all I ever want to say about it, ever again.

★ ★ ★

MELISSA: Mr. and Mrs. Darwin H. Cobb announce the birth of their daughter Francesca . . .

ANDY: Many congratulations on the baby.

MELISSA: Harvard Law School yet! Are you getting all stuffy and self-important?

ANDY: As you know, I've always liked to write letters. I decided I might do better trying to write laws, which, after all, are the letters that civilization writes to itself.

MELISSA: Yes you ARE getting all stuffy and self-important. Come and have a drink with us some time. We're right on the way to New York. And sooner or later everyone comes to New York.

ANDY: Read the *New York Times* account of your show in Stamford. Sounds like you are causing a series of seismic shocks up and down the Merritt Parkway . . .

MELISSA: Don't joke about my work. There's more there than what they said in your goddamn BIBLE, *The New York Times*. Enclosed see what OTHER critics said. Notice they think I'm GOOD! I AM, too! Or could be. If I can only FOCUS . . .

ANDY: Sorry, sorry, sorry. I know you're good. I've always known it.

★ ★ ★

MELISSA: Hear you made Law Review, whatever that means. I assume you review laws. I wish you'd review some of the marriage laws . . .

ANDY: Just a quick note. Are you in any trouble?

MELISSA: I don't understand your last note. We're fine. All fine. Everyone's fine.

★ ★ ★

ANDY: Congratulations on baby number two . . .

MELISSA: Number two is a perfect way to describe this particular baby . . .

ANDY: Greetings from Washington. Here clerking for a Supreme Court Justice which isn't quite as fancy as it sounds . . .

★ ★ ★

MELISSA: Dear Andy: I was very sorry to hear about the death of your father. I know he was a great influence on you, and I know you loved him very much. I also know he didn't like *me*. I'm sure he thought I was bad for you, and I probably was. Still, he was a good, decent man, and I always knew where I stood with him when you'd bring me home to your family, back in the old days, back in the Land of Oz. I wish I'd had a father like that. Please accept my deepest sympathies. Love, Melissa.

ANDY: Dear Melissa. Thank you for your note on my father. I did love him. He was a classy guy, the best of his breed. Even now he's gone, I can still hear him reminding me of my obligations to my family, my country, and myself, in roughly that order. All my life, he taught me that those born to privilege have special responsiblities, which is I suppose why I came home alone from Japan, why I chose the law, and why I'll probably enter politics at some level, some time on down the line. Thanks for writing. Love, Andy.

★ ★ ★

MELISSA: Merry Christmas. I'm enclosing a snapshot mother took of me and the girls. Don't I look domestic? Stop looking at my hair! By the way, you'll notice you-know-who is not in the picture.

ANDY: Thanks for the Christmas card. Are you in trouble?

MELISSA: Greetings from Reno. Could I stop by Washington on the way back East?

ANDY: Let me know when you're coming. You can meet Jane.

MELISSA: Jane?

ANDY: I'm going out with a great girl named Jane.

★ ★ ★

MELISSA: Melissa Gardner Cobb regrets that she will be unable to accept the kind invitation of . . .

ANDY: Dear Melissa: Had to add my two-cents worth to Jane's thank-you note for the wedding present. (Guess who is jealousy peeking over my shoulder to make sure this isn't a love letter.) First of all, thanks for the present, whatever it was. Ah, a tray! I am now told it was a tray. A *hand-painted* tray. Hand-painted by you, I'll bet. Anyway, thank you. I hope all goes well with you, as it does with us. We'll be moving to New York in the fall. I've got a job with one of those high-powered law firms. It will probably be stuffy as hell for a while, but I'll learn the ropes. Besides, it's in my home state and might be a good jumping-off place for something political a little way down the line. We BOTH want you to come to dinner once we're settled in. And don't say you never come to New York. Sooner or later everyone comes to New York, as someone once wrote me, long, long ago.

★　★　★

Merry Christmas from us to you. Where are you these days?

★　★　★

Happy Birthday. See? Even a married man never forgets.

★　★　★

Get well soon. Mother wrote that you had had some difficulty. I hope it's not serious, and by now you're feeling fine.

★　★　★

I can't remember exactly what one dozen red roses are supposed to say, but here they are, and I hope they say, "cheer up."

★   ★   ★

Hey! I sent you some flowers a while back. Did you receive them? Are you all right?

★   ★   ★

MELISSA: Dear Andy. Yes, I'm all right. Yes, I got your flowers. Yes, I'm fine. No, actually, I'm not fine, and they tell me I've got to stop running around saying I am. I'm here at this posh joint outside Boston, drying out for one hundred and fifty-five dollars a day. One of my problems is that I got slightly too dependent on the Kickapoo joy juice, a habit which they tell me I picked up during the party days back in Our Town. Another is that I slide into these terrible lows. Mummy says I drag everybody down, and I guess she's right. Aaaanyway, the result is that my EX has taken over custody of the girls, and I'm holed up here, popping tranquilizers, talking my head off in single and group psychiatric sessions, and turning into probably the biggest bore in the greater Boston area.

ANDY: Have you thought about doing some painting again? That might help.

★   ★   ★

Did you get my note about taking up art? You were good, and you know it. You should keep it up.

MELISSA: I *did* get your note, I *have* taken it up, and it *helps*. Really. Thank you. I'm channeling my rage, enlarging

my vision, all that. I hope all goes well with you and—
wait, hold it, I'm looking it up in my little black book
. . . ah hah! Jane! It's Jane. Hmmmm. I hope all's well
with you and Jane.

ANDY: Merry Christmas from Andy and Jane Ladd. And
Andrew the Fourth! Guess the name of the dog.

MELISSA: Porgy.

ANDY: You got it.

* * *

MELISSA: Merry Christmas from San Antonio. Am trying
the Southwest. I can see the most incredible shapes from
my bedroom window. And there's also a pretty incredible shape now sleeping in my bed.

ANDY: Seasons Greetings from the Ladd family. (Mother
wrote you were planning to get married again.)

MELISSA: I was. I did. I'm not now.

ANDY: Donner, Rhodes and McAlister announce the appointment to partnership of Mr. Andrew M. Ladd, III . . .

MELISSA: Dear Andy: Now you're such a hotshot lawyer,
could you help me get my children back? Darwin hardly
lets me near them, and when he does, they behave as
if I had some contagious disease. I wasn't much of a
mother, but maybe I could improve, if I just had the legal
responsibility . . .

ANDY: Better stay out of this one . . . Our past connections
. . . conflict of interest . . .

MELISSA: Hello from Egypt. I'm trying to start again in the
cradle of civilization.

* * *

ANDY: Christmas Greetings from the Ladds: Andy, Jane,
Drew, Nicholas, and Ted. And of course Porgy.

MELISSA: Am thinking of moving to Los Angeles. Do you know anyone in Los Angeles? Does anyone know anyone in Los Angeles?

★ ★ ★

ANDY: Joy to the World from all the Ladds. Note our new address.

MELISSA: Merry Christmas. Hey you! What's going on? Just when I decide to move to New York, I see you've scampered off to the suburbs.

ANDY: I find the suburbs generally safer.

MELISSA: Chicken.

★ ★ ★

Mother wrote that you won some important election for the Republicans. I'm terribly disappointed. I love all politicians, but I find Democrats better in bed . . .

ANDY: I'm a liberal Republican with a strong commitment to women's rights. Doesn't that count?

MELISSA: Depends on your position.

★ ★ ★

MELISSA: Paintings and drawings by Melissa Gardner. The Hastings Gallery. 422 Broadway. March 18 through April 30. Opening reception March 20, 6 to 8 P.M. Note I've gone back to my *maiden* name. That's a laugh

ANDY: Got you announcement for your new show. Good luck. P.S. I'd love to have one of your paintings. We could use a little excitement on our living room walls. Seriously. What would one cost?

MELISSA: Come to the show and find out.

ANDY: Never made your show. Sorry. Things came up.

MELISSA: Chicken again.

ANDY: You're right.

MELISSA: Actually, it's just as well. I'm going through what the critics call an "anarchistic phase." They say I'm dancing on the edge of an abyss. You'd better stay away. I might take you with me when I fall.

★ ★ ★

ANDY: Dear Friends: Jane tells me that it's about time I took a crack at the annual Christmas letter, so here goes. Let's start at the top, with our quarterback, Jane herself, who never ceases to amaze us all. Not only has she continued to be a superb mother to our three sons, but she has also managed to commute into the city and hold down a part-time job in the gift shop at the Metropolitan Museum of Art. Furthermore, she is now well on her way to completing a full-fledged master's degree in Arts Administration at SUNY-Purchase. More power to Jane, so say we all.

We are also proud of all three boys. Young Drew was soccer captain at Exeter last fall, and hopes to go on to Yale. Nicholas, our rebel in residence, has become a computer genius in high school, and has already received several tantalizing offers for summer jobs from local electronics firms. We all know that it's tougher to place our youngsters in meaningful summer employment than to get them into Harvard, so we're very proud of how far Nick has come. Ted, our last but in no way our least, now plays the clarinet in the school band at Dickinson Country Day. Since Jane and I are barely capable of singing "You Are My Sunshine" without going disastrously flat, when we hear him produce his dulcet sounds, we look at each other "in a wild surmise."

We recently bought the family summer place from my brother and sister, and hope to spend as much time as we can there, gardening, relaxing, and as the boys say, "generally veging out." Jane and I have become killers on the tennis court, and hereby challenge all comers. If any of our friends are in the Adirondack area this summer, we expect telephone calls, we expect visits, we expect elaborate house presents.

I've enjoyed very much serving on the state legislature. We've proposed and written a number of bills, and we've won some and lost some. All my life I've had the wish to do something in the way of public service, and it has been a great pleasure to put that wish into practice. For those of my friends who have urged me to seek higher office, let me simply say that I have more than enough challenges right here where I am.

Jane and the boys join me in wishing each and all of you a Happy Holiday Season.

MELISSA: Dear Andy. If I ever get another one of those drippy Xeroxed Christmas letters from you, I think I'll invite myself out to your ducky little house for dinner, and when you're all sitting there eating terribly healthy food and discussing terribly important things and generally congratulating yourselves on all your accomplishments, I think I'll stand up on my chair, and turn around, and moon the whole fucking family!

ANDY: You're right. It was a smug dumb letter and I apologize for it. Jane normally writes it, and it sounds better when she does. I always felt better writing to just one person at a time, such as to you. I guess what I was really saying is that as far as my family is concerned, we're all managing to hold our heads above water in this tricky world. Jane and I have had our problems, but we're comfortable with each other now, and the boys, for the moment, are out of trouble. Nicky seems to be off drugs now, and Ted is getting help on his stammer. Porgy, Jr., my old cocker, died, and I miss him too much to get a replacement. I'm thinking of running for the Senate next fall if O'Hara retires. What do you think? I'd really like your opinion. If you decide to answer this, you might write care of my office address. Jane has a slight tendency toward melodrama, particularly after she got ahold of your last little note.

MELISSA: The Senate yet! I should have known. Oh Andy, just think! Once again, you can be with all boys. Oh hell, go for it, if you want. You'll be an image of righteousness and rectitude in our godforsaken land. Or maybe it's just me that's godforsaken these days.

ANDY: The Honorable Andrew M. Ladd, III, wishes to express his thanks for your generous donation to his senatorial campaign . . . You sent too MUCH, Melissa! You didn't need to.

★ ★ ★

MELISSA: Greetings from Silver Hill. Slight regression in the liquor department. They say it's in the genes. Lord knows, my mother has the problem, and my father, too, in the end. Anyway, I'm working on it. Darwin is being a real shit about the girls. He's cut down on my visitation rights, so when you get to Washington, I want you to write a special law about vindictive ex-husbands, banishing them to Lower Slobbovia, forever and ever. Amen.

★ ★ ★

ANDY: Season's Greetings from Senator and Mrs. Andrew M. Ladd and family.

MELISSA: Season's Greetings indeed! Is that all you can say to me after forty years? I'm warning you, Andy. Keep that shit up, and I swear I'll come down and moon the whole Senate.

ANDY: Sorry. My staff sent that out. Merry Christmas, old friend. How are you? Where are you these days?

MELISSA: Living in New York—alone, for a change—but the big question is, WHO am I these days? That's the toughie. I keep thinking about that strange old world we grew up in. How did it manage to produce both you and me? A stalwart upright servant of the people, and a boozed-out, cynical, lascivious old broad. The best and the worst, that's us.

ANDY: Don't be so tough on yourself. Get back to your art.

MELISSA: I'll try.

★ ★ ★

ANDY: Merry Christmas, Happy New Year, and much love.

MELISSA: Much LOVE? MUCH love? God, Andy, how sexy! Remember how much that meant in our preppy days? If it was just "love" you were out in the cold, and if it was "all my love," you were hemmed in for life—but "much love" meant that things could go either way. Remember?

★ ★ ★

ANDY: Merry Christmas and love from us all.

MELISSA: Saw you on *Sixty Minutes*. You looked fabulous. And that was a great little pep talk in the Senate on "our responsibilities" to Latin America. But don't forget to keep your eye on the ball.

ANDY: Thanks for your card. What ball?

MELISSA: The ball is that money doesn't solve everything. It helps, but not as much as people think. Take it from one who knows. That's the ball.

* * *

ANDY: Merry Christmas and love. What are you up to these days?

MELISSA: I'm trying to work with clay. Remember that kind of clay we used in Mrs. Mickler's art class in fourth grade? That old gray stuff? We called it plasticene. I'm trying to work with that. I'm making cats, dogs . . . I even made a kangaroo jumping over a glass of orange juice. Remember that? I'm trying to get back to some of those old, old feelings I had back in the Homeland. I have to find feelings, any feelings, otherwise I'm dead. Come down and help me search. I have a studio down in Soho and we could . . . um, er, uh, well we could at least have DINNER and talk about old times, couldn't we, Senator Ladd? P.S. Did you know that my mother got married again? At the age of eighty-two? To my father's BROTHER yet! So now you have to call her Mrs. Gardner again, just like the old days. The wheel seems to be coming around full circle. Hint, hint.

ANDY: A quick note on the way to the airport. When you write, put "attention Mrs. Walpole" on the envelope. She's my private secretary, I've alerted her, and she'll pass your letters directly to me. Otherwise, the whole office staff seems to get a peek. In haste . . .

MELISSA: I'm having a show opening January 28 through Feb. 25. Won't you come? I'd love to have you see what I've been up to. Maybe it will ring a few old bells.

ANDY: Can't make it. I'll be on an official visit to the Philippines most of February, then a week's spring skiing at Stowe with the boys. Good luck.

* * *

How did the show go?

* * *

Haven't heard from you. Tell me about the show.

* * *

I want to hear from you, Please.

MELISSA: The show stank. The crowd hated it, the critics hated it, I hated it. It was nostalgic shit. You can't go home again, and you can quote me on that. I'm turning to photography now. Realism! That's my bag. The present tense. Look the modern world squarely in the face, and don't blink . . . Oh Andy, couldn't I see you? You're all I have left.

ANDY: I'll be in New York next Tuesday the 19th. Have to make a fund-raising speech at a dinner. I could stop by your place afterwards.

MELISSA: I'll be there all evening.

* * *

ANDY: Red roses. This time I think I know what they mean.

MELISSA: All I know is that after last night I want to see you again.

* * *

Any chance of any other fund-raisers coming up in the near future?

* * *

Mrs. Walpole, are you there? Are you delivering the mail?

* * *

ANDY: I'm sorry I've taken so long to reply. I've been upstate mending a few fences, and then to Zurich for a three-day economic conference, and then a weekend with Jane, mending a few fences *there* . . . Darling, I'll have to ask you not to telephone the office. Every call has to be logged in, and most of them get screened by these overeager college interns who like to rush back to Cambridge and New Haven and announce to their classmates in political science that Senator Ladd is shacking up on the side. The phones simply aren't secure. At long last, the letter beats out the telephone, my love! And guess what? I'm writing this with the old Parker 51 my grandmother gave me when I went away to school. I found it in the back of my bureau drawer with my Scroll and Key pin, and my Lieutenant J.G. bars from the Navy, and the Zippo lighter you gave me at some dance. The pen didn't even work at first. I had to clean it out, and then traipse all over Washington looking for a store which still sells a bottle of ink. Anyway, it feels good holding this thing again. It feels good writing to you again. Longhand. Forming my *d*'s and *t*'s the way Miss Emerson taught us so long ago. I know you've never liked writing letters, but now you HAVE to! Ha, ha. As for business: I plan to come through New York next Wednesday, and I'll call you from the airport if there's time to stop by.

MELISSA: Sweetheart, I LOVED seeing you. Come again . . .

ANDY: . . . will be stopping through a week from next . . .

MELISSA: . . . Did you ever *dream* we'd be so good at sex?

ANDY: . . . Two up-tight old Wasps going at it like a sale at Brooks Brothers . . .

MELISSA: . . . I figure fifty years went into last night . . .

ANDY: . . . Let's go for a hundred . . .

MELISSA: . . . Oh my god, come again, soon, or sooner . . .

ANDY: . . . I'm already making plans . . .

MELISSA: . . . have to go to San Francisco to visit the girls. Couldn't we meet somewhere on the way?

ANDY: . . . I don't see how we can possibly go public . . .

MELISSA: . . . some country inn, some deliciously seedy motel . . .

ANDY: . . . I don't see how . . .

MELISSA: . . . see you more than for just a few hours . . .

ANDY: . . . price we have to pay . . .

MELISSA: . . . I'm getting so I think about nothing but how we can . . .

ANDY: . . . I'm not sure I can change my whole life so radically . . .

MELISSA: . . . other politicians have gotten divorced . . . Rockefeller, Reagan . . .

ANDY: . . . Jane . . . the children . . . my particular constituency . . .

MELISSA: . . . you've become the center of my life. If you left, I don't think I could . . .

ANDY: . . . because of the coming election, I don't see how we can . . .

MELISSA: Dear Andy: A reporter called up from the *Daily News*. What do I do about it?

ANDY: Nothing.

MELISSA: I suppose you know all this, but there's a crack about us in *Newsweek*. And Mother heard some radio talk show where they actually named names. What should I do? Go away? What?

ANDY: Nothing.

MELISSA: They called Darwin, you know. They tracked him down. The son of a bitch told them this had been going on for years.

ANDY: Wish it had been.

MELISSA: Now they're telephoning. What do I say?

ANDY: Say we're good old friends.

MELISSA: Friends, I like. Good, I like. Old, I'm beginning to have problems with.

ANDY: Then don't say anything. Hang up. This, too, shall pass.

MELISSA: Will I be seeing you again?

ANDY: Better not, for a while.

MELISSA: I meant, after the election . . .

ANDY: Better lie low for a while.

MELISSA: I miss you terribly . . .

ANDY: Better lie low.

MELISSA: I NEED you, Andy. You're my anchor man these days. Without you, I'm not sure I can . . .

ANDY: Hold on now. Just hold on . . .

MELISSA: . . . where were you? I waited three hours hoping that you'd at least call . . .

ANDY: . . . please don't telephone . . . Mrs. Walpole was sick that day and . . .

MELISSA: . . . I haven't seen you in over a month now . . .

ANDY: . . . the coming election . . .

MELISSA: . . . surely you could at least take time out to . . .

ANDY: . . . if I want to be reelected . . .

MELISSA: . . . I need you. I need to be with you. I don't know if I can . . .

ANDY: . . . the election . . . the election . . . the election . . .

★   ★   ★

MELISSA: I haven't heard from you in six weeks, Andy.

★   ★   ★

Are you trying to tell me something, Andy?

★   ★   ★

Is this it, Andy?

* * *

Congratulations on landslide victory. Love. Melissa.

ANDY: Could we meet at your place next Sunday night?
MELISSA: Oh thank God . . .
ANDY: I meant that we have to talk, Melissa . . .
MELISSA: Uh oh. Talk. I'm scared of talk. In fact, I dread
  it . . .

* * *

ANDY: Dearest Melissa: Are you all right? That was a heavy
  scene last Sunday. But I know I'm right. We've got to go
  one way or the other, and the other leads nowhere. I know
  I sound like a stuffy prick, but I do feel I have a responsibility to Jane, and the boys, and now, after the election,
  to my constituency, which had enough faith and trust in
  me to vote me back in despite all that crap in the newspapers. And it wouldn't work with us anyway, in the long
  run, sweetheart. We're too old. We're carrying too much
  old baggage on our backs. We'd last about a week if we
  got married. But we can still write letters, darling. We can
  always do that. Letters are still our strength and our salvation. Mrs. Walpole is still with us, and there's no reason
  why we can't continue to keep in touch with each other in
  this wonderful old way. I count on your letters, darling. I
  always have. And I hope you will count on mine . . .

* * *

Are you there? I keep putting "please forward" on the
envelopes but who knows . . .

* * *

Now I've even resorted to the telephone, but all I get is your damn machine . . . Please. I need to hear from you . . .

* * *

Senator and Mrs. Andrew M. Ladd, III, and family send you warm Holiday greetings and every good wish for the New Year.

MELISSA: Andy Ladd, is that YOU? Blow-dried and custom-tailored and jogging-trim at fifty-five. Hiding behind that lovely wife with her heels together and her hands folded discreetly over her snatch? And is that your new DOG, Andy? I see you've graduated to a golden retriever. And are those your sons and heirs? And—Help!—is that a *grand*child nestled in someone's arms? God, Andy, you look like the Holy Family! Season's Greetings and Happy Holidays and even Merry Christmas, Senator Ladd. We who are about to die salute you . . .

ANDY: Just reread your last note. What's this "we who are about to die" stuff?

* * *

May I see you again?

* * *

I want to see you again, if I may.

* * *

Dear Mrs. Gardner. I seem to have lost touch with Melissa again. I wonder if you might send me her latest address.

* * *

Dear Melissa. Your mother wrote that you'd returned to the Land of Oz. I'm flying up next Thursday to see you.

MELISSA: No! Please! Don't! Please stay away! I've let myself go. I'm fat, I'm ugly, my hair is horrible! I'm locked in at the funny farm all week, and then Mother gets me weekends if I'm good. They've put me on all sorts of new drugs, and half the time I don't make sense at all! I can't even do finger-painting now without fucking it up. My girls won't even *talk* to me on the telephone now. They say I upset them too much. Oh, I've made a mess of things, Andy. I've made a total, ghastly mess. I don't like life any more. I hate it. Sometimes I think that if you and I had just . . . if we had just . . . oh but just stay away, Andy. Please.

ANDY: Arriving Saturday morning. Will meet you at your mother's.

MELISSA: DON'T! I don't want to see you! I won't be there! I'll be GONE, Andy! I swear. I'll be gone.

* * *

ANDY: Dear Mrs. Gardner: I think the first letter I ever wrote was to you, accepting an invitation for Melissa's birthday party. Now I'm writing you again about her death. I want to say a few things on paper I couldn't say at her funeral, both when I spoke, and when you and I talked afterward. As you may know, Melissa and I managed to keep in touch with each other most of our lives, primarily through letters. Even now, as I write this letter to you, I feel I'm writing it also to her.

MELISSA: Ah, you're in your element now, Andy . . .

ANDY: We had a complicated relationship, she and I, all our lives. We went in very different directions. But somehow over those years, I think we managed to give something to each other. Melissa expressed all the dangerous and rebellious feelings I never dared admit to . . .

MELISSA: *Now* he tells me . . .

ANDY: And I like to think I gave her some sense of balance . . .

MELISSA: BALANCE? Oh hell, I give up. Have it your way, Andy: balance.

ANDY: Most of the things I did in life I did with her partly in mind. And if I said or did an inauthentic thing, I could almost hear her groaning over my shoulder. But now she's gone I really don't know how I'll get along without her.

MELISSA: *(Looking at him for the first time.)* You'll survive, Andy . . .

ANDY: I have a wonderful wife, fine children, and a place in the world I feel proud of, but the death of Melissa suddenly leaves a huge gap in my life . . .

MELISSA: Oh now, Andy . . .

ANDY: The thought of never again being able to write to her, to connect to her, to get some signal back from her, fills me with an emptiness which is hard to describe.

MELISSA: Now Andy, stop . . .

ANDY: I don't think there are many men in this world who have had the benefit of such a friendship with such a woman. But it was more than friendship, too. I know now that I loved her. I loved her even from the day I met her, when she walked into second grade, looking like the lost princess of Oz.

MELISSA: Oh, Andy, PLEASE. I can't bear it.

ANDY: I don't think I've ever loved anyone the way I loved her, and I know I never will again. She was at the heart of my life, and already I miss her desperately. I just wanted to say this to you and to her. Sincerely, Andy Ladd.

MELISSA: Thank you, Andy.

THE END

The Golden Age

The Golden Age was first presented at the Greenwich Theatre, in London, in the spring of 1980. It was directed by Alan Strachan, with the following cast:

VIRGINIA .... Angela Thorne
TOM .... Vincent Marzello
ISABEL .... Constance Cummings

It was somewhat revised, and produced in the fall of 1983 at the Kennedy Center, in Washington, D.C., by Roger Stevens and Ralph G. Allen. It was directed by John Tillinger; the set was by Oliver Smith; the lighting by Arden Fingerhut; and the costumes by Jane Greenwood. This same production opened at the Jack Lawrence Theatre, in New York City, in April 1984, produced by Nicholas Benton, Stanley Flink, and Brent Peek. The cast was as follows:

VIRGINIA .... Stockard Channing
TOM .... Jeff Daniels
ISABEL .... Irene Worth

(The play was first done as a staged reading at The Aspen Playwrights Conference in 1979, with Barbara Babcock, Peter Maloney, and Celeste Holm, directed by William Shorr.)

CAST

VIRGINIA
TOM
ISABEL HASTINGS HOYT

Time: Spring and summer, today

Setting: The front room of the second floor of a brownstone
house on the upper East Side of New York

Suggested by a story of Henry James

The room should be presented on enough of an angle so
that we see at least part of a front window, and an entrance
from the hall, where we may also see a section of the
staircase, leading up to other rooms, and down to the kitchen,
dining room, and front door. Dominating the room, however, Upstage, should be a large archway, leading to the
back section of this floor. The archway has heavy dark red
plush curtains, to be easily opened and closed.

The room is filled with fine old antique furniture. The walls
are covered with paintings—oils, still lifes, etchings, and
prints. The effect should be one of cluttered, complicated
old elegance.

ACT I

AT RISE: The room is empty. The light from the window suggests afternoon, late spring. The curtains for the Upstage archway are closed.
After a moment, voices of a man and a woman are heard from the Left—the ad-lib chatter of two people coming up the stairs.
VIRGINIA comes in from the Right. She is a plain, rather awkward woman, simply dressed, probably in a sweater and skirt. There's something vague about her, and something nervous. She glances around the room, at the closed curtains particularly, and then turns, back toward the hall.

VIRGINIA: Come in.
  (TOM comes in from the hall. HE is a nice-looking guy, youngish, well-dressed. HE has a camera slung over his shoulder, like a tourist. HE looks around.)
TOM: *(Enthralled)* Oh boy.
VIRGINIA: I know it.
TOM: Fabulous room.
VIRGINIA: This is the front room.
TOM: *(Indicating curtains)* And through there is . . . what?
VIRGINIA: The back room.
TOM: Oh. Right.
VIRGINIA: No, actually, it was the library.
TOM: Was?
VIRGINIA: She had it done over.
TOM: The lady who lives here?

VIRGINIA: Exactly. She had slipcovers made for all the books.

TOM: No.

VIRGINIA: No. I'm teasing. *(Pause)* She had it made into her bedroom.

TOM: Ah.

VIRGINIA: She even has a bathroom in there, and a dressing room in back, so she can be all on one floor.

TOM: I see. You mean, because she's so . . .

VIRGINIA: So what?

TOM: Well, I mean, isn't she quite . . .

VIRGINIA: Quite what?

TOM: Well. Old.

VIRGINIA: Not at all! *(Pause)* Oh she says she is, but she really isn't. *(Pause)* I keep telling her she's ageless. She's as beautiful as ever, and she's got a mind like a steel trap. *(Pause)*

TOM: I'd like to meet her.

VIRGINIA: Who wouldn't?

TOM: Could I?

VIRGINIA: Oh no.

TOM: I couldn't?

VIRGINIA: Out of the question. She's given up meeting people.

TOM: Why? Are they too much for her?

VIRGINIA: No. She's too much for them. Now she won't even read her mail. She makes me send it back.

TOM: I know.

VIRGINIA: You wrote her?

TOM: Twice. They both came back unopened.

VIRGINIA: There you are.

(TOM shrugs, looks around.)

TOM: Great stuff, anyway.

VIRGINIA: The loot?

TOM: The furniture.

VIRGINIA: She calls it her loot.

TOM: Well, it's great old stuff.

VIRGINIA: Do you think we're a little cluttered?

TOM: Oh no.

VIRGINIA: She keeps saying how cluttered we are.

TOM: I like it.

VIRGINIA: She says this is what you get when you've owned five houses.

TOM: Five?

VIRGINIA: At one time.

TOM: No.

VIRGINIA: Yes.

TOM: May I ask where?

VIRGINIA: Oh gosh. Let me think. There was this, of course, here in New York. And one out in Long Island. And one in the Adirondacks, for the fishing. That's what? Three. Oh, and one in South Carolina. I don't know. Anyway, five.

TOM: And everything ended up here?

VIRGINIA: Oh not everything. Just what didn't get away.

TOM: I see.

VIRGINIA: She says she's a dark star.

TOM: A what?

VIRGINIA: A dark star. She read this article in the *New York Times* Magazine Section which said that when a universe collapses, all these *things* collect around a dark star.

TOM: Oh yes?

VIRGINIA: You can't even see the star, but you know it's there, because all these things keep gravitating to it.

TOM: Hmmm.

VIRGINIA: Like this furniture. *(Pause)* And me. *(Pause)* And now you.

(Pause. HE looks at her.)

TOM: And you're the housekeeper.

VIRGINIA: Sort of.

TOM: Personal secretary, then.

VIRGINIA: Sort of that, too.

TOM: Companion? Nurse?

VIRGINIA: Not *nurse*. She doesn't need a *nurse*. *(Pause)* No, actually, I'm her granddaughter.

TOM: *Grand*daughter?

VIRGINIA: That's what I am.

TOM: You mean, she's your *grand*mother?

VIRGINIA: Absolutely.

TOM: Wow.

VIRGINIA: I know it.

TOM: Hmm. And you stop by during the day?

VIRGINIA: I live here.

TOM: All the time?

VIRGINIA: All the time.

TOM: Just you and she.

VIRGINIA: Just us. Oh, we had a cat. But it got away.

TOM: You do the shopping and cooking and stuff?

VIRGINIA: Try to.

TOM: She's lucky.

VIRGINIA: Why?

TOM: To have you. In this day and age.

VIRGINIA: Why?

TOM: I mean her own granddaughter.

VIRGINIA: I'm lucky to have her.

TOM: Oh. Sure.

VIRGINIA: Well. You've seen the downstairs, and you've seen this. Now you'd better go.

TOM: What if you told her I was writing an article? About these old brownstones?

VIRGINIA: Oh she knows that.

TOM: Knows it?

VIRGINIA: She guessed. When I told her you were at the door, and wanted to see the house, she said you probably wanted to write something.

TOM: What else did she say?

VIRGINIA: Oh just . . . show him in. Show him around.
And show him out. *(Pause)*

TOM: That's what she said, huh?

VIRGINIA: That's what she said. So shall we go?

TOM: *(Indicating camera)* May I at least take a picture?

VIRGINIA: No.

TOM: Just one picture.

VIRGINIA: I said no.

TOM: Just to have something to hold on to.

VIRGINIA: Please.

TOM: Look, I can't just walk away from this.

VIRGINIA: Oh there are plenty of other brownstones in New
York.

TOM: I'm not only interested in the house.

VIRGINIA: You're not?

TOM: No. I'm interested in what it contains.

VIRGINIA: You mean, the loot?

TOM: No, I'm interested in the . . . aura.

VIRGINIA: The aura?

TOM: The mystery. The magic. There are echoes here.
Glimmerings of a golden age. I'm ultimately interested in
. . . something else.

*(The curtains part to reveal a spectacular old woman standing in
the archway.)*

ISABEL: He's ultimately interested in me.

VIRGINIA: Gram! I thought you wanted to stay out of it.

ISABEL: Well now I've decided to get into it.

TOM: *(Exultantly)* I knew you were still alive!

ISABEL: Well at least I try to give that general effect.

VIRGINIA: *(Going to her)* Gram, this is . . .

ISABEL: Don't bother to introduce us. I'll forget his name.
He already knows mine.

TOM: Well I . . .

ISABEL: Of course you do. You've looked me up. *(Pause)*

TOM: Isabel Hastings Hoyt.

ISABEL: *(Majestically holding out her hand)* How do you do. *(TOM goes to shake it.)* Be careful. It's an antique.

TOM: I'm really glad to meet you, Mrs. Hoyt.

ISABEL: You should be. I'm a rare bird. It must be like shaking hands with a whooping crane.

VIRGINIA: Where would you like to sit, Gram?

ISABEL: I seem to be heading toward that chair. *(SHE begins to make her way D. toward a particular chair.)*

VIRGINIA: Would you like some help, Gram?

ISABEL: No thank you. I'm still afloat. Just throw me a line if I miss my mooring. *(To TOM, as she moves by him)* I feel like the old *Mauretania*, dragged out of mothballs. I need paint, I'm listing to starboard, I probably leak. But I'm still operating under my own steam.

VIRGINIA: You certainly are, Gram.

ISABEL: Oh yes. I'm still able to slide into a slip. *(SHE waves VIRGINIA away.)* Without tugs. Without a pilot. *(SHE reaches her chair.)* There. Now. All engines reverse. *(SHE backs up, settles into her chair.)* Ah. *(To VIRGINIA)* Now you can add a few fenders. *(VIRGINIA props her up with pillows. To TOM.)* And if you think that was complicated, wait till I try to get up.

VIRGINIA: Oh Gram, you're marvelous.

ISABEL: Virginia, dear girl, that light. Can you move it? There's no point in having me look as if I were sitting in the dentist's chair. Unless this man is a dentist. Are you a dentist, sir?

VIRGINIA: *(Moving the light a little)* He's a writer, Gram. Remember?

ISABEL: He can be both. Everyone writes these days. Including dentists. *(To TOM)* Are you serious about your writing?

TOM: I want to be, Mrs. Hoyt.

ISABEL: *(To* VIRGINIA*)* Is he fun to be with? Is he bright and amusing?

VIRGINIA: I haven't noticed, Gram.

ISABEL: Then he's not really serious. *(To* TOM*)* You're a—graduate student.

TOM: I used to be. But I gave it up.

ISABEL: I don't believe you. I can smell an academic a mile away.

TOM: Oh well, I teach a course on American literature three nights a week at Hunter College.

ISABEL: *(To* VIRGINIA*)* You see?

TOM: But that's just to make ends meet.

ISABEL: Oh I don't like academics. They're all so hungry.

TOM: Some of them are pretty well fed these days.

ISABEL: For life, man. They're hungry for *life.* They suck your blood. Which would finish me, since I have very little left.

VIRGINIA: Oh Gram . . .

ISABEL: Now a real writer brings *in* life. He creates it.

TOM: That's why I want to be one. That's why I've come to New York.

ISABEL: Then do it, man! On your own! Don't lean on an old woman!

VIRGINIA: *(Low to* TOM*)* Maybe you'd better go.

ISABEL: When I want people to go, I tell them, which is one of the few advantages of being old.

VIRGINIA: All right, Gram.

ISABEL: And I'm still not in love with that light. *(To* TOM*)* Irene Castle always kept the light a little to her left. She felt it made her look more beautiful.

VIRGINIA: *(Moving the light again)* Don't talk so much, Gram. You'll get tired.

ISABEL: It's where you keep putting that light. There's a writer here. Please try to keep me reasonably mysterious. Like the Oracle of Delphi.

VIRGINIA: *(Adjusting the light once again)* I'll try, Gram.

ISABEL: *(To* TOM*)* I met her, you know.

TOM: Irene Castle?

ISABEL: The Oracle of Delphi.

VIRGINIA: Oh Gram . . .

ISABEL: *(Insistently)* I met the Oracle. On a trip to Greece with the Van Dusens. They wanted to consult her about the stock market. It was stupid of them. They had no sense of history. Neither did the Oracle. She gave them all the wrong tips.

VIRGINIA: Ssshhh. You're all wound up.

ISABEL: I am, aren't I? I feel like some bit of fluff out of Booth Tarkington, all dizzied up for the first date. Go make us a drink.

VIRGINIA: I'll make tea, Gram.

ISABEL: Tea? For a writer? Real writers like liquor.

VIRGINIA: At four in the afternoon?

ISABEL: At four in the morning. *(To* TOM*)* What kind of drink would you like, sir?

TOM: *(Looking from one to the other)* Oh I don't really . . .

ISABEL: *(To* VIRGINIA*)* Make him a Brandy Alexander. Make me one, too.

VIRGINIA: I don't know how to make Brandy Alexanders, Gram.

ISABEL: Then learn. Read a book. Read Hemingway's *A Moveable Feast*. He describes one in there.

VIRGINIA: Oh Gram . . .

ISABEL: Or at least he describes something which sounds absolutely delicious. Make whatever it is he describes.

VIRGINIA: Gram, what are you up to?

ISABEL: I am getting you out of the way, dear girl, so I can put this man on the spot.

VIRGINIA: Oh Gram . . .

ISABEL: Without you saying "Oh Gram" every other minute. Now go. Shoo. Goodbye.

(VIRGINIA *goes off, toward downstairs and kitchen, very reluctantly.* ISABEL *is suddenly all business.*)

Pull up that chair where I can see you.

TOM: All right.

ISABEL: Now sit in it.

(TOM *does. She looks him over.*)

A writer, eh?

TOM: Hope to be.

ISABEL: Were you a bad teacher?

TOM: No, I was good. Last year I won a teaching prize for my "contagious enthusiasm." (ISABEL *laughs.* TOM *adds embarrassedly.*) Quote unquote.

ISABEL: In what subject?

TOM: American literature. Mid-twentieth century. What I call the Golden Age.

ISABEL: Why are you giving it up?

TOM: Oh I'm not. Really. I just want to dig deeper. I want to be where it was. I want to look at things more directly.

ISABEL: Seems odd you'd want to start by writing gossip.

TOM: Oh, hey, listen: I intend to make this a big article.

ISABEL What makes you think you'll get anything big from me?

TOM: Because you knew some of the finest writers of your time, Mrs. Hoyt, and I figure if I can get closer to them, work with them, work with you, then I'll be able to connect. (*Pause*)

ISABEL: How did you turn me up?

TOM: Well ever since I came to town, I've been poking around the Twenties collection in the New York Public Library. And I keep coming across your name.

ISABEL: My name was bandied about.

TOM: It sure was.

ISABEL: I'm in several books.

TOM: So I discovered.

ISABEL: I'm in the index of two.

TOM: Yes.

ISABEL: Out of print, I suppose. Most of them.

TOM: All of them.

ISABEL: I'm not in paperback?

TOM: Not you.

ISABEL: I would have loved to be in paperback. Think of being taken on the bus, carried to the beach.

TOM: I can't see it, Mrs. Hoyt. You're hardback, all the way. *(Pause)*

ISABEL: Did you find out much about me, from these books?

TOM: Not much. They kept a respectful distance.

ISABEL: They put me at most of the parties.

TOM: Yes.

ISABEL: I was there.

TOM: I'm sure you were.

ISABEL: And I gave the best ones, by far.

TOM: I read about them . . .

ISABEL: Am I still in the Social Register?

TOM: They list you as dead.

ISABEL: Those stinkers! That's because I refused to subscribe.

TOM: You're listed as dead there, and dead one other place, but I couldn't find an obituary in the *Times*.

ISABEL: I'd be in the *Times*. Certainly I'd be there.

TOM: I know, Mrs. Hoyt. So I was at a loss where to turn next.

ISABEL: You probably decided I was babbling away in some nursing home.

TOM: I did. I almost gave up on you.

ISABEL: Faint heart ne'er won fair lady.

TOM: I know. And then I came across your picture.

ISABEL: Where?

TOM: In the old *Life* magazine.

ISABEL: Ah. The old *Life* . . .

TOM: *(Indicating archway)* You were standing in that doorway, waving goodbye.

ISABEL: I remember. I was giving a party for Scott Fitzgerald before he went back to France. Some photographer got wind of it.

TOM: In the picture, were you waving goodbye to Fitzgerald?

ISABEL: I was not. I was waving goodbye to the photographer. I was saying, "Scram, please. This is a private party." Which I ought to say to you.

TOM: Well all I know is you looked absolutely spectacular in that dress.

ISABEL: I did, didn't I?

TOM: And that kept me going.

ISABEL: But where? How did you find the house? I never gave out the address, and the telephone's unlisted.

TOM: Ah well. A few weeks ago at Hunter we were doing *Moby Dick*. And a student came up with the mailing list for Save The Whales.

ISABEL: Oh the whales, those poor whales. I give them five dollars every Christmas.

TOM: So it said. And there was your address.

ISABEL: And here you are. To harpoon me.

TOM: Oh no. Just to tell the world what it's been missing. *(Pause)*

ISABEL: Help me up. I want to stagger majestically around the room. *(TOM helps her up, stays standing himself.)* Thank you. *(SHE walks, turns, looks at him.)* Are you a pansy?

TOM: No!

ISABEL: Be frank.

TOM: I'm not, Mrs. Hoyt.

ISABEL: Too bad. It's the pansies who have good taste.

TOM: Oh I've got good taste. Why do you think I'm here?

ISABEL: All right. Let's see if you do. What do you think is the best thing here?

TOM: The best?

ISABEL: The very best. My most prized possession.

TOM: Let me look.

ISABEL: Yes. You look.

(HE *looks around.* SHE *watches him.*)

TOM: This cabinet looks pretty good.

ISABEL: The doors are fake.

TOM: Fake?

ISABEL: Look inside. You'll see new wood.

TOM: How about this chair?

ISABEL: Just a copy.

TOM: I'm surprised.

ISABEL: I like fake things. They're stronger. You can use them. You can sit on them. And you don't feel so badly when they break.

TOM: Is everything here fake?

ISABEL: Not at all.

TOM: There are some good things?

ISABEL: The best. Open your eyes.

TOM: *(As* HE *moves around)* Am I getting warmer?

ISABEL: No.

TOM: Then I give up.

ISABEL: You've seen it. You've looked right at it.

TOM: I'm sorry.

ISABEL: I'll give you a hint. The best thing here is downstairs.

TOM: In the front hall?

ISABEL: In the kitchen.

TOM: In the kitchen?

ISABEL: Trying to make Brandy Alexanders. *(Pause)*

TOM: Oh. Of course.

ISABEL: By far the best thing I possess.

TOM: Right. Oh sure. *(Pause)*

ISABEL: Well I have to decide whether to let you into my life. You're attractive, but at my age that's not supposed to make much difference. Tell me one more thing about yourself that will absolutely bowl me over.

TOM: *(Carefully)* I come from Saint Paul, Minnesota. *(Pause)*

ISABEL: I don't believe you.

TOM: It's true. *(Pause)*

ISABEL: Scott Fitzgerald came from Saint Paul, Minnesota.

TOM: He's my favorite author. I identify with him completely. *(Pause)*

ISABEL: I knew him quite well.

TOM: That's why I'm here. *(There is the sound of something breaking, Off R. TOM notices it; ISABEL doesn't seem to.)*

ISABEL: Well you'd better go.

TOM: Go?

ISABEL: Go.

TOM: But what about our Brandy Alexanders?

ISABEL: See if you can survive without one.

TOM: But she's down there, making them.

ISABEL: She's down there, drinking them. *(Another louder crash Off L.)* The Golden Sauce. One of the things that has come down to us from the Golden Age.
(She hoists herself out of her chair.)

TOM: You mean she . . .

ISABEL: I mean that dear girl has a slight difficulty with the bottle.

TOM: Then why did you let her start?

ISABEL: As if I could make her stop . . . Now hurry down the hall, and you won't embarrass her.

TOM: Couldn't I . . . ?

ISABEL: No you couldn't. Please go.

TOM: *(Taking his raincoat)* But what about the article?

ISABEL: *(Drawing herself up)* Article, sir? Do you think for one minute I would let you write a magazine article?

TOM: You wouldn't?

ISABEL: I would not. I am worthy of an entire *book!* *(Pause)*

TOM: I'll come back tomorrow.

ISABEL: That would be fine. *(SHE waves him Off, watches him disappear down the stairs. We hear the outside door slam. Then SHE walks slowly toward the hall, calling softly.)* Vir-

ginia . . . Virginia . . . See if you can make coffee, please
. . . We have things to discuss.

*(The lights fade. Music comes up, preferably the old Paul
Whiteman recording of "Poor Butterfly."* As the light comes
up, we hear the sound coming from an old Capehart gramophone
somewhere in the room. After a moment, VIRGINIA comes in
from the hall, in a less frumpy dress. SHE looks around, as if to
make sure the coast is clear, then calls Off.)*

VIRGINIA: Come in.

(TOM comes in, carrying a bunch of flowers.)

TOM: Thank you.

(HE looks around for Isabel.)

VIRGINIA: I turned on the Victrola just to get you in the
mood. It's "Poor Butterfly"—Gram's favorite song.

TOM: Oh.

VIRGINIA: Are you in the mood now?

TOM: Yes.

VIRGINIA: Then I'll turn it off. *(Turning off the victrola)*
Would you like something to drink? Tea? Coffee? Or a
Brandy Alexander?

TOM: No thanks. This is a working day.

VIRGINIA: Yes. The situation is slightly different from yesterday, isn't it?

TOM: Oh yes.

VIRGINIA: Your reception, and everything.

TOM: I'll say.

VIRGINIA: Today you're getting the red carpet treatment.

TOM: Seems so. *(Remembering flowers)* Oh I brought these.

VIRGINIA: They're lovely! . . . For Gram?

TOM: For—both of you.

VIRGINIA: *(Takes them)* I'll take them in. *(Starts for curtains,
then stops)* Oh. Gram asked me to call your attention to

*See Special Note on copyright page.

that painting. You might look at it while I'm gone. *(SHE indicates an oil portrait on the wall.)*

TOM: This?

VIRGINIA: It's somebody famous.

TOM: Who?

VIRGINIA: Guess.

TOM: Hmmm . . . A nude study . . . of a male.

VIRGINIA: Focus on the face.

(SHE goes out through the curtains with the flowers. HE studies the painting. SHE comes back in.)

She says thank you for the flowers.

TOM: She's very welcome . . . *(Indicating the painting)* Who is this? The face is vague.

VIRGINIA: I think it's Fitzgerald.

TOM: No!

VIRGINIA: I think it is.

TOM: You *think?* You *think* your *grand*mother owns a portrait of F. Scott Fitz*gerald* in the *nude?*

VIRGINIA: I think she painted it.

TOM: *Painted* it? Her*self?*

VIRGINIA: Oh she painted lots of famous people. She has this studio up on the fourth floor. Where she painted.

TOM: I don't believe it. Fitzgerald would never have posed in the nude. He was a very fastidious guy.

VIRGINIA: Then maybe it's Walter Babcock McCoy.

TOM: Who's Walter Babcock McCoy?

VIRGINIA: Don't you know?

TOM: Doesn't ring a bell.

VIRGINIA: I think he wrote plays.

TOM: Sounds like old melodramas.

VIRGINIA: That's it. Rip-roaring melodramas.

TOM: And he posed for her.

VIRGINIA: Everybody did.

TOM: Except Fitzgerald.

VIRGINIA: Ask her.

TOM: I will. I intend to. *(Pause.* HE *glances toward the curtains.)* As soon as she comes out.

VIRGINIA: Oh she's not.

TOM: Not coming out?

VIRGINIA: Not today.

TOM: Why? She's not sick, is she?

VIRGINIA: She's *fine*. She's perfectly fine. She just doesn't want to see you until we've established some ground rules.

TOM: Ground rules?

VIRGINIA: She says whenever you have a working relationship, it's a good idea to spell things out from the word Go.

TOM: Spell things out.

VIRGINIA: Otherwise, she says there's bound to be trouble. Once, on Long Island, she brought in this man to work around the house, and she forgot to spell things out, and he managed to ruin all the plumbing.

TOM: Hey, I'm not a plumber!

VIRGINIA: That's the point. Neither was the man.

TOM: *(Glancing toward curtains)* All right. Ground rules.

VIRGINIA: *(Producing a piece of blue note paper)* Actually, she gave me this list.

TOM: A list.

VIRGINIA: As you know, as I think she may have told you, I have a slight . . . problem. I have this tendency to . . . retreat. And she thinks I should learn to deal with things more directly.

TOM: O.K. Fine. Let's do it.

VIRGINIA: All right. Now. The first thing she writes, in capital letters, is HOW MUCH.

TOM: How much?

VIRGINIA: *(Showing him the list)* See? Capital letters. "HOW MUCH." *(Pause)*

TOM: Oh. How much do I want to *know*.

VIRGINIA: No, that's not it. Because there's a little dollar sign here. After the HOW MUCH. Isn't that a little dollar sign? I think it is.

TOM: So she means how much . . .

VIRGINIA: Money. *(Pause)*

TOM: She means how much . . .

VIRGINIA: Will you pay.

TOM: For what?

VIRGINIA: For what she gives you. *(Pause)*

TOM: Is she serious?

VIRGINIA: I think she is.

TOM: I haven't thought about money.

VIRGINIA: Well she has. *(Pause)*

TOM: Well, what does she suggest?

VIRGINIA: Suggest?

TOM: On that list.

VIRGINIA: Oh. *(SHE refers to the list.)* She writes fifty.

TOM: Fifty dollars.

VIRGINIA: Fifty percent.

TOM: Of *what?*

VIRGINIA: Of what you make. From your book.

TOM: *(Laughing)* Would you tell her I don't even have a publisher yet?

VIRGINIA: Oh she knows that. This is for when you get one.

TOM: Fifty percent . . . That's quite a chunk . . .

VIRGINIA: She says this will be a major best seller.

TOM: How does she know?

VIRGINIA: Because she knows the world. And she knows books. And she knows what the world wants to read in books.

TOM: *(Shrugging tolerantly)* O.K. Fine. We split the pie fifty-fifty. Let's hope.

(VIRGINIA checks off that item on her list, moves on to the next.)

VIRGINIA: All right. Next. She writes "Advance."

TOM: Advance?

VIRGINIA: She wants an advance.

TOM: *(Laughing)* She does, does she? How much?

VIRGINIA: Ten thousand dollars.

TOM: Ten thousand *dollars*?

VIRGINIA: Before she opens her mouth.

TOM: That's ridiculous.

VIRGINIA: She says Gloria Swanson got twice that.

TOM: She knows I don't have ten thousand dollars.

VIRGINIA: She knows a publisher does.

TOM: I don't *have* a publisher.

VIRGINIA: Then go *get* one.

TOM: How can I just *get* one?

VIRGINIA: You can tell them what you've got.

TOM: What have I got?

VIRGINIA: You've got *her*, when she's got ten thousand dollars.

TOM: *(Getting up; exasperatedly)* Oh look, Miss . . . Miss . . .

VIRGINIA: Please call me Virginia.

TOM: All right, Virginia, look . . .

VIRGINIA: And can I call you . . . what?

TOM: Tom. The name's Tom. Look . . .

VIRGINIA: I mean it's silly not to. We're going to be seeing a lot of each other.

TOM: *(Driving through)* Look. Virginia! Please! No publisher is going to look at me unless I've got something concrete. Tell your grandmother that, please.

VIRGINIA: Oh she knows that. She's not dumb.

TOM: Well then what's she got to *show* for her ten thousand dollars?

VIRGINIA: That painting, for one thing.

TOM: Which is a nice amateur portrait of some man . . .

VIRGINIA: It's not amateur!

TOM: . . . who wrote old plays . . .

VIRGINIA: It's a first-rate painting!

TOM: All right, it's terrific. But it's not Fitzgerald. And it's not worth ten thousand dollars.

VIRGINIA: She *realizes* that. *(SHE opens a worn Manila folder.)* That's why I'm supposed to show you this . . . And this . . . and this . . .
(SHE lays out a series of documents on the coffee table between them, as if she were trumping him in bridge.)

TOM: What are those!

VIRGINIA: She says read 'em and weep.
(TOM picks up the documents one by one.)

TOM: A postcard . . . Depicting an old sailing schooner . . . *(Reads the other side)* Signed "Joseph C." . . . "Dear Isabel: Thank you for an immensely reinvigorating weekend. I will always remember sitting on your veranda, under a vast swarm of stars, watching the small boats bobbing on the bay . . ." *(Looks at her)* Joseph C?

VIRGINIA: She says the ship is significant.
(Pause. HE turns over the card.)

TOM: Joseph *Conrad?*

VIRGINIA: I think so.

TOM: You *think* so? You think she may have reinvigorated Joseph Conrad?

VIRGINIA: May have.

TOM: *(Looking at next document)* A sheet of music . . . a score sheet . . .entitled "Isabel" . . . *(Reads the lyrics)* "Isabel . . . I wish you well, my love . . . but what the hell, my love. *(HE looks at her.)* Sounds like Cole Porter.

VIRGINIA: That could be it.

TOM: Your *grand*mother has a *lost* song written about her by Cole Porter?

VIRGINIA: She said there's something on the back.

TOM: *(Looking on the back)* With additional lyrics by T. S. Eliot.

VIRGINIA: That's it.

TOM: *(Shaking his head)* I don't believe this.

VIRGINIA: Don't, then.

(SHE *gathers up the remaining items.*)

TOM: Wait. *(She stops.)* What else is there?

VIRGINIA: You won't believe it.

TOM: Give me a chance. I'll . . . try.

(SHE *looks at him, then slowly hands him another photograph; he looks at it carefully*)

A small man . . . And a big woman . . . By a pool . . .

(HE *looks at her, looks at photograph again.*)

I want to say it's . . . Calvin Coolidge and Edith Wharton! In bathing suits!

VIRGINIA: Then say it.

TOM: These faded old photographs. It's hard to tell. He seems . . . to be . . . goosing her.

VIRGINIA: I think he is.

TOM: Calvin Coolidge is goosing Edith Wharton?

VIRGINIA: Apparently they had this game . . .

TOM: *(Now on his feet, holding the documents)* But *Jesus!* This stuff is fabulous.

VIRGINIA: You see? You see what I'm talking about?

TOM: Does she have any stuff on Fitzgerald? Any of his writings, for example. There's supposed to be some lost things he wrote when he was in New York.

VIRGINIA: Then she might have it.

TOM: Might?

VIRGINIA: Now don't distract me. I'm supposed to talk about money. She says none of those things, separately, is worth a huge amount. But you put them together, and you add all the other things she has—why then you have your Golden Age. And any decent publisher will want to pay for it.

TOM: *(Poring over documents)* This is incredible . . .

VIRGINIA: *(Returning to her list)* Now here's where I get very confused. She wrote down all these things like "movie sales" and "television specials," and she wants to be out in a nice, cheap paperback within the year.

TOM: Never mind! I agree to it all! *(Gathering up documents, starting for the door)* Let me get cracking, then!

VIRGINIA: No! Wait! *(SHE holds out her hand.)* She wants those things back. Nothing is to leave this house.

TOM: Why not?

VIRGINIA: Because people will steal it and copy it.

TOM: Look, I'll keep a tight watch.

VIRGINIA: *(Determinedly, holding out her hand)* She doesn't want Edith Wharton Xeroxed. Particularly in a bathing suit.

TOM: Look, I swear—

VIRGINIA: *(Shaking her head)* Think of the Pentagon Papers. May I have them back, please?

TOM: But how will the publishers *know?*

VIRGINIA: She says you can *tell* them. Verbally. Using words. *(HE hands them back.)*

TOM: But they won't believe me.

VIRGINIA: Tell them to trust you. As we do. Tell them the Golden Age, like all great civilizations, was based on trust. *(SHE takes the photographs and puts them back into the folder.)* And then tell them to make out a cashier's check for ten thousand dollars.

TOM: Look, Virginia, I may be new in town, but I know it won't work.

VIRGINIA: Won't work?

TOM: I won't get a nickel out of any publisher unless I have something specific in hand.

VIRGINIA: Oh yes. Here. Show them this. *(SHE produces another piece of blue note paper.)*

TOM: *(Reading)* "To whom it may concern. This man is writing a book about me. It will be worth at least ten thousand dollars up front." Signed, Isabel Hastings Hoyt.

VIRGINIA: She said that should do it. And this. *(SHE hands him a photograph.)*

TOM: *(Looking at it)* Her picture. From the old *Life*. Waving goodbye.

VIRGINIA: Isn't she lovely? It's my favorite, of all the snapshots.

TOM: This is the picture that cheered me on.

VIRGINIA: Then it should cheer on the publishers, too. Tell them as soon as she gets that check, she'll sing like a canary.

TOM: *(Putting the note and picture in his pocket)* I'll tell them she's waving goodbye to Fitzgerald. That might open a few doors.

VIRGINIA: Or else you might mention Walter Babcock McCoy.

TOM: Who? *(Glances at painting)* Oh right.

VIRGINIA: Good. Just wait, then, while I tell Gram it's a deal.

TOM: One thing, Virginia.

VIRGINIA: *(Stopping)* What?

TOM: I have to say this: I'm amazed the way she likes money.

VIRGINIA: She *hates* money. She thinks money is the root of all evil!

TOM: Well, she sure likes to rake it in.

VIRGINIA: That's because she needs it!

TOM: Come on! She must be sitting on a small fortune.

VIRGINIA: She doesn't have a nickel.

TOM: With this house? This furniture?

VIRGINIA: It's not *hers*!

TOM: What??

VIRGINIA: She's in hock up to her elbows!

TOM: I don't believe you.

VIRGINIA: It's true! Everything here is tied up in some dumb historical trust . . .

TOM: But still, the income . . .

VIRGINIA: . . . lasts only as long as she lives!

TOM: O.K., but . . .

VIRGINIA: Oh you dope! Don't you *see?* She wants the money for *me!*

TOM: For you?

VIRGINIA: *(Voice breaking)* She's decided she's dying . . . And she wants me taken care of after she's gone . . .

(SHE turns and exits through the curtains. TOM stands amazed, and then goes out as the lights dim. Lights come up on ISA-BEL, entering through the curtains, carrying a teetering stack of old shoe boxes. It is late afternoon.)

ISABEL: Now here are some more, since you didn't like the last batch. God knows what's in them, but they're from the twenties.

(SHE sets boxes on chaise and discovers TOM isn't in the room. SHE starts to the hall looking for him.)

Where are you?

(TOM comes in from the hall, with a portable tape recorder.)

TOM: I thought we'd try this again. It might help you focus.

ISABEL: On what?

TOM: The Golden Age.

(ISABEL crosses to chaise, sits and starts going through the shoe boxes. TOM sits on the footstool and sets up the recorder.)

ISABEL: I don't see why you want to call your book *The Golden Age.* It's a cliché, after all. Everyone's always using it. The Golden Age of this, The Golden Age of that. The other day I heard a man on the news talking about the Golden Age of television. *(SHE laughs.)*

TOM: I don't care. It's what I want.

ISABEL: Just because it's gone doesn't mean it's golden. Those awful wars, that ghastly depression . . .

TOM: I'm thinking of the time between.

ISABEL: You think the twenties were golden?

TOM: For some. For you.

ISABEL: What makes you say that?

TOM: Because you still shine, Mrs. Hoyt.

ISABEL: And you are a charmer, sir.

(*ISABEL might wear reading glasses, and uses a magnifying glass as she sifts through things. TOM, in more informal clothes, sits close to her, holding a microphone for a tape recorder.*) All right. Let's focus on the Twenties. (*SHE pokes among her boxes.*) The Twenties . . . the Twenties . . . (*SHE finds a box. SHE shuffles through the box.*) Aiken . . . Locust Valley . . . New York. Let's concentrate on New York.

TOM: O.K.

ISABEL: (*Taking out a letter*) Here is a letter signed, I think it's "L," from someone who is apologizing for spilling the soup.

TOM: Who was "L"?

ISABEL: I have no idea. I remember the soup. I don't remember who spilled it. It could have been Lawrence.

TOM: D. H. *Lawrence?*

ISABEL: D. H. or T. E. One of the two. No, it wasn't, T. E. He went back to Arabia. It might have been Gertrude.

TOM: Gertrude Lawrence spilled the soup?

ISABEL: Oh dear, I don't know. The point is the soup. And someone is sorry for spilling it. Actually, they shouldn't be sorry, whoever it was. We had a lot of soup. And a lot of spillings. I think we all spilled so much because we drank so much. We had to. We had such terrible soup. We had these miserably unhappy Irish cooks whom we'd drag along from house to house, winter and summer. They weren't interested in soup. Neither were we. So they'd make it, and we'd spill it. And of course when we did, there would be a rather standard pattern. The women would shriek, the men would groan, chairs would scrape, the maids would cluck. There would be all this dabbing with napkins. And all sorts of insane suggestions about what to do with the tablecloth. People would throw salt on it, and champagne, and send to the kitchen for baking soda. It made an absolute mess. No one would settle down till the salad, and even during the dessert— *(SHE stops, eyes the microphone.)* I can't go on.

TOM: You're getting tired?

ISABEL: *(Indicating the microphone)* No, no, it's that thing. I can't stand it being pointed at me. Particularly at my mouth. I'm never quite sure where it's been.

TOM: All right.

(HE turns off the recorder.)

I'll take notes.

(HE picks up a notebook and pencil.)

Go on.

(Pause)

ISABEL: Now I've lost the thread. You see? You see what happens? You try to record things, to pin them down, and you lose them completely. It's called the Hindenberg Effect. Or the Hawthorne Effect. I knew Hindenberg. He had an excellent cook. I never knew Hawthorne, of course, but I imagine his food was abominable. *(Pause)* Oh dear. Now I'm completely lost.

TOM: You were right in the middle of dessert.

ISABEL: Let's leave the table, and go to another room.

TOM: Tell me about Fitzgerald.

ISABEL: Tell me about your wife.

TOM: I don't have a wife.

ISABEL: I'll bet you did. In Minnesota.

TOM: That's ancient history.

ISABEL: So is Fitzgerald.

TOM: Mrs. Hoyt . . .

ISABEL: Fair's fair. We used to have a rule on Long Island. Eleanor Roosevelt made it up. If one person went skinny-dipping, everyone did.

TOM: *(Writing again)* Eleanor Roosevelt went skinny-dipping?

ISABEL: Only at night. And only when William Faulkner wasn't there.

TOM: Why wouldn't she do it with Faulkner?

ISABEL: I don't know. It had something to do with his position.

TOM: His position?

ISABEL: On the Negroes, dear boy. I don't know. I've forgotten . . .

TOM: *(Putting down his pencil)* Mrs. Hoyt, do you realize how frustrating this is?

ISABEL: Frustrating?

TOM: Everything you tell me kind of peters out . . . Everything is full of vague possibilities which don't materialize.

ISABEL: That's life, dear boy. That's how it goes.

TOM: Mrs. Hoyt, let me remind you of something. I'm working on spec here. Do you understand what that means? I am *speculating* on you. I'm not getting a nickel for doing this. Nothing. No publisher has been willing to cough up one red cent until we produce something tangible and concrete. And what's happening? You won't let me take anything out of the house, and you won't give me anything serious to write about, and you get dicey when I even ask. Now I'm *betting* on you, Mrs. Hoyt. I'm putting my life on the line here. I came to New York, and I tracked you down, and I dug you *up*, because I think you've got something to tell the world, Mrs. Hoyt. And what do you give me? A lot of broad, unsubstantiated talk about spilled soup and skinny-dipping! Jesus, Mrs. Hoyt, you are letting me *down! (Pause)*

ISABEL: I've been naughty, haven't I?

TOM: Yes you have.

ISABEL: I'll try to be a good girl.

TOM: Thank you.

ISABEL: At least I'll do the best I can.

TOM: Thank you very much.

ISABEL: Then, as they say, shoot.

TOM: Tell me about Fitzgerald.

ISABEL: Oh poor, dear Fitzgerald. Don't you think he's been pretty well pawed over by now?

TOM: I'm not sure, Mrs. Hoyt. Some scholars think there are pieces of his writing yet to be discovered.

ISABEL: Really . . .

TOM: Things he wrote in New York. Around the time you knew him.

ISABEL: Mercy . . .

TOM: In fact, you know what I think?

ISABEL: Tell me . . .

TOM: I think there may be a whole section of *The Great Gatsby* lying around somewhere.

ISABEL: Heavens.

TOM: That's what I think. There's a gap in that book, Mrs. Hoyt. Every time I teach it, I sense it. There's a lost chapter . . . a section . . . even a paragraph which would make the whole thing hang together.

ISABEL: Ah. And if you found that, you'd really strike gold, wouldn't you?

TOM: It would be the answer to a dream. So anything you can tell me about Fitzgerald might help. *(Pause)*

ISABEL: Are you interested in a long-lost romance?

TOM: Yes!

ISABEL: Between a great writer and an impressionable young girl?

TOM: Yes. Oh yes. That's it! Tell me all about it.

ISABEL: Well. I met him when I was on tour with Maud Adams.

TOM: You were once an actress?

ISABEL: Once and always, sir. And apparently I was so enchanting that he asked me to star in his new play.

TOM: You mean there's a long-lost play?

ISABEL: Well it's long, but it's not lost. I have several copies.

TOM: Of a play? By Fitzgerald?

ISABEL: Fitzgerald? Who said anything about Fitzgerald? I've been talking about Walter Babcock McCoy. *(Pause)*

TOM: Oh.

ISABEL: You've heard of him?

TOM: Oh sure.

ISABEL: He was a wonderful playwright. We used to call him the real McCoy.

TOM: The real McCoy . . .

ISABEL: He wrote these marvelous melodramas, full of exciting scenes which never meant anything. Oh I adored him. There is no love like the first love.

TOM: But there must have been others.

ISABEL: Oh well, there was one. But I hate to talk about him.

TOM: Because it's so painful?

ISABEL: Because it's so boring. He was my husband.

TOM: *(Disappointed again)* Oh.

ISABEL: Roger Hoyt. He promised me the moon if I'd leave the stage and marry him.

TOM: So you did . . .

ISABEL: Well I married him, but I never left the stage. I simply learned to play another part.

TOM: The loving wife?

ISABEL: Exactly! And Roger was marvelous—in the supporting role. Together we put on a splendid show.

TOM: But it wasn't enough . . .

ISABEL: Well I thought it was. Until I remembered something.

TOM: You remembered you were a woman.

ISABEL: I remembered I was a mother.

TOM: I forgot there were children.

ISABEL: So did I. But we had two. And we hired various sympathetic souls to take care of them. Then one day, after I had finished painting, and Roger had come in from hunting, I said, "Roger, where are the children? We have these children somewhere. We should be seeing them."

TOM: What did he say?

ISABEL: He said, "You're quite right." So we arranged a time. We had them all gussied up and trotted in. And there we all were. Eyeing each other. It was ghastly.

TOM: So what did you do?

ISABEL: I got a game.

TOM: Game?

ISABEL: I got a game. I said to Roger, "You play games, I play games, these children should play games."

TOM: What did he say?

ISABEL: He said, "You're quite right again." So I sent away to Schwartz. "Help. For heaven's sake, send me a game." And when the children came in, I said, "Here, children. Here's a game. Play it." But then, oh dear, they began to argue. And I said, "Children, don't fight, don't argue. Just play the game." Finally Roger said, "If you children don't stop fighting, I'm leaving this room." But they didn't. So he did.

TOM: He walked out of the room?

ISABEL: He walked out of the house.

TOM: You mean, he left?

ISABEL: Forever.

TOM: My God, you must have felt absolutely defeated.

ISABEL: I felt absolutely delighted. He gave me a handsome settlement, and we'd meet occasionally for lunch in New York.

TOM: And now you were free.

ISABEL: As a bird.

TOM: Enter Fitzgerald, am I right? *(Pause)* Mrs. Hoyt? *(No answer)* Would you at least tell me what happened to your husband? And the children?

ISABEL: They died.

TOM: How?

ISABEL: I don't want to talk about it anymore.

TOM: Please, Mrs. Hoyt . . .

ISABEL: I don't. And I won't.

TOM: So I can't write a book about any of that?

ISABEL: No you can't.

(VIRGINIA *comes in, carrying a cat.*)

VIRGINIA: Look what Virginia dragged in.

ISABEL: Good heavens.

VIRGINIA: I was planting myrtle in the garden and there it was. It came back.

ISABEL: So it did.

VIRGINIA: But isn't it amazing? It survived the whole winter.

ISABEL: Someone else probably took care of it.

VIRGINIA: Maybe.

(*Going out*)

Or maybe it got along by it*self.* I'll give it some milk.

(SHE *goes off,* R.)

ISABEL: (*Shaking her head*) Not the same cat.

TOM: What?

ISABEL: Not the same cat at all. That's an entirely different cat.

TOM: You're sure?

ISABEL: Of course. I know a cat when I see one. (*Pause*) But I hope *you* noticed something just then, sir.

TOM: Noticed what?

ISABEL: Something besides that cat.

TOM: Such as what?

ISABEL: For example, I hope you noticed the time.

TOM: (*Checking his watch*) Four-thirty in the afternoon.

ISABEL: And guess who isn't wandering around the house with a glass in her hand at four-thirty in the afternoon.

TOM: (*Looking toward* L.) You're right.

ISABEL: And guess who's putting things into the garden.

TOM: It's great, it's wonderful.

ISABEL: And guess who's looking more relaxed and calm and beautiful with every passing day. People notice her on the street now. Last week a masher approached her in the grocery store.

TOM: Really?

ISABEL: Oh yes. It's all very exciting. Are you in love with your wife?

TOM: Me?

ISABEL: You. Do you plan to go back to her?

TOM: We don't get along any more.

ISABEL: Why not?

TOM: She says I roll around in books like a dog in dead fish.

ISABEL: Sounds like a very graphic lady.

TOM: She says I'm lost in the lost generation. Maybe she's right. Maybe I'm so much in love with the past that I can't love anything else. *(Pause)*

ISABEL: Oh dear.

TOM: Yes, well I don't like the present very much, Mrs. Hoyt. I think we're a greedy, vulgar society and we're spinning out of control. Now you stood in the doorway of something different, Mrs. Hoyt. You guarded it, Fitzgerald wrote about it, and there was something *there*! *(Pause)*

ISABEL: Would you like me to tell you something Fitzgerald never mentions?

TOM: Sure.

ISABEL: All right. I'll look back through this doorway, and tell you what *I* see behind me.

TOM: Go ahead.

ISABEL: First, of course, I see one hell of a good party.

TOM: Yes. Fitzgerald saw that.

ISABEL: Oh yes. And he saw that behind every good party is a woman.

TOM: Now we're cooking . . . a beautiful woman . . .

ISABEL: No, not a beautiful woman, a smart woman. And behind that woman was money.

TOM: Fitzgerald saw all that.

ISABEL: But that's where he stopped. He never saw that behind the money was always something else.

TOM: A lover?

ISABEL: A list.

TOM: *(Looking up)* A what?

ISABEL: A list. I believe you've seen my lists.

TOM: I believe I have.

ISABEL: Well then you should know that behind the Golden Age was a good long list. Of things for other people to do. Buy this, serve that, plant this, fix that. With one good list, we could juggle two, three, five houses in the air, without skipping a beat. We could equip and feed and move an army without losing a mitten. With lists in hand, we crossed rivers, scaled mountains, and established civilizations which lasted all summer long . . . *(Pause)* And behind these lists . . . Would you like to know what was behind these lists?

TOM: Yes I would.

ISABEL: Behind these lists were the slaves.

TOM: The slaves?

ISABEL: The slaves, the slaves. Those poor half-literate Irish girls stumbling up the backstairs after midnight, setting their alarms for the crack of dawn. Those dogged English grooms, already up to curry and saddle those horses we decided not to ride. Those glorious Italians, continually weeding the gardens. The Polish laundress, the German who fixed the pump for the pool, the Scottish nurse—oh those people, those dear people. They made your Golden Age, my dear. They built it from the bottom up. They came in through the Golden Door and they kept the whole thing going. They're not in those boxes, and they won't be in your book, but they were there, all through it. Oh heavens! Oh mercy! I remember them all! Alice and Jean and Vito and Mrs. Veele. I remember them, more and more. I dream of them. Who did we think we were? What did we think we were doing? Bossing those people around.

TOM: You're a regular Marxist, Mrs. Hoyt.

ISABEL: I don't know what I am. I do know we made unconscionable use of other people.

TOM: Oh but hell, Mrs. Hoyt. We do that today. It's always done. All civilizations rest on the backs of somebody's labor.

ISABEL: Maybe so. But no civilization likes to know about it. Which is why I want you to write a good, easy, chatty book which will sit on every coffee table in the country, and make us all a great deal of money.

TOM: Fitzgerald would never have settled for that.

ISABEL: Oh well. Fitzgerald . . .

(VIRGINIA comes in from the hall, carrying a tray and a glass of medicine.)

VIRGINIA: Are you getting tired, Gram? Remember what the doctor said.

ISABEL: It's rather nice to forget.

(SHE toasts Tom with the medicine, then drinks it.)

VIRGINIA: Well I'm starting your dinner. We'll have to eat a little early if we're going to watch the Yankee game.

ISABEL: All right, dear.

(VIRGINIA goes out; ISABEL watches her. TOM is forced to. Finally.)

Have you met a nice girl since you've come to town?

TOM: Actually yes.

ISABEL: Some student in class? Batting her eyes

TOM: No actually, a teacher. She does a course on the Brontës, right down the hall.

ISABEL: The Brontës? Oh dear. That means you're terribly involved.

TOM: I was, Mrs. Hoyt. But lately things are petering out.

ISABEL: Why?

TOM: I don't know . . . To be honest, Mrs. Hoyt, I'm kind of hung up on you. *(Pause)*

ISABEL: I'll tell you three more things before I make my exit.

TOM: Good.

ISABEL: Things which are not for publication. Things which are private. Things which have to do with feelings.

TOM: O.K.

ISABEL: First, I'll tell you what happened to my husband.

TOM: Roger?

ISABEL: I don't believe you were ever introduced.

TOM: Mr. Hoyt, then.

ISABEL: Thank you. He was murdered.

TOM: Murdered?

ISABEL: Oh we didn't call it that in those days. We called it a hunting accident. He went hunting with the Vice President of the United States, and the Vice-President shot Roger.

TOM: No.

ISABEL: Yes. It seems they both had feelings about the same chorus girl. Apparently the Vice-President's feelings were stronger.

TOM: Boy.

ISABEL: The second thing: my children. The older—a boy—was drowned in a sailing accident off Northeast Harbor. He had feelings of independence. He liked to be alone in the water, and in the end, he was.

TOM: I'm sorry.

ISABEL: The other—a lovely girl—had feelings of inferiority. "Don't be silly," I'd say. "Go out. Have fun." So she tried. She went to a party after the war, and met a soldier. Nine months later she produced Virginia. They say the war ended the depression. Not for her it didn't. Not by a long shot . . . And would you like to know my own feelings about all of this?

TOM: No need, Mrs. Hoyt.

ISABEL: Then I'll simply tell you this. When the war was over, I retired. Totally and completely. I didn't like what I saw behind me, and I certainly didn't like what I saw coming up.

(SHE gets up.)

I'm now making a farewell appearance just to get money.
(SHE starts for her room.)

TOM: *(Getting up)* But you said there were three things.

ISABEL: *(Going to the hall, looking up the stairs)* I happen to
have a studio on the top floor.

TOM: I know.

ISABEL: It has a bed, a desk, and its own bath. Fitzgerald
stayed there.

TOM: Did he?

ISABEL: Would you like to stay there while you write our
book?

TOM: Of course!

ISABEL: Fine. Move in any time you want.

TOM: Thank you very much!

ISABEL: But that's not the third thing.

TOM: Not the third thing?

ISABEL: This Brontë woman . . . Are you sure you're no
longer running her around the moors?

TOM: I'm sure.

ISABEL: Then the third thing is written on that blue piece of
paper on the table by the hall.

TOM: *(Hurriedly crossing, picking up the paper, reading aloud)*
Angelo de Vita. 310 West 46th Street. *(Looks at her)* Does
he have something to do with Fitzgerald?

ISABEL: He does not. He is the owner of a nice little Italian
restaurant on the West Side. His father—no, his *grandfather*—used to be our gardener, and when he retired, I
gave him some money so his children could make a fresh
start. Now you go downstairs, and tell that lovely girl to
stop cooking, and put on a pretty dress, and come out to
dinner with you at Angelo's. And tell Angelo to send me
the bill. And order the soup. Angelo makes good soup.
(SHE starts in.)

TOM: Mrs. Hoyt—

(SHE stops, turning in the doorway.)

Did Fitzgerald write anything in the studio?

ISABEL: Oh yes.

TOM: Do you have what he wrote?

ISABEL: Oh yes.

TOM: Is it . . . important?

ISABEL: Everything Fitzgerald wrote is important. But so is the soup. So don't spill it. Good night.

(SHE goes out through the curtains. TOM stands looking after her, then exits into the hall.)

END OF ACT I

ACT II

Night, as indicated from the window. One light is on in the room, and a light in the hall. Voices, as VIRGINIA and TOM come up the stairs. VIRGINIA comes in and turns on another light. SHE now looks very pretty, in a pretty dress. TOM wears the same clothes.

VIRGINIA: Here kitty, kitty, kitty.

TOM: *(In doorway)* Maybe it's still downstairs.

VIRGINIA: It adores Gram.

TOM: She doesn't seem to reciprocate.

VIRGINIA: Oh phooey. She just gets mad because it won't always do what she wants. *(Looks at him)* Anyway, come in.

TOM: *(Coming in hesitantly; indicating the curtained area)* Won't we wake her up?

VIRGINIA: Oh no. She sleeps like a top. Come on.
(SHE turns on another light.)
That was fun.

TOM: Nice little restaurant. Good food.

VIRGINIA: Which you weren't supposed to pay for.

TOM: I like to think I can pick up a tab.

VIRGINIA: Well she'll be furious. She'll insist on writing you out a check.

TOM: Why?

VIRGINIA: She just will. She wants the whole evening to be on her.

(SHE finds another piece of blue note paper on a table.)
Oh look, she even left this.

TOM: A list?

VIRGINIA: Just a note. *(Reads)* "Brandy in the cabinet, cigars in the humidor."
(Turns to him)
Have some brandy and cigars.

TOM: No thanks.

VIRGINIA: *(Going to highboy)* Oh come on. It's fabulous brandy. I ought to know.

TOM: No, really.
(VIRGINIA brings out a brandy bottle and a large snifter on a silver tray.)

VIRGINIA: If you're worrying about me, don't, that's all. I'm fine. I got through cocktails without a cocktail, didn't I? I got through dinner without wine. I can certainly get through the rest of the evening watching a good man enjoy good French brandy.

TOM: O.K.
(SHE pours him a snifter.)

VIRGINIA: Guess who gave her this?

TOM: Who?

VIRGINIA: Trotsky.

TOM: Back off.

VIRGINIA: Yes he did. One winter, she rented a villa in Cuernavaca so they could argue politics, and he brought her a case of brandy as a house present.
(Hands it to him.)
Here. Have some of Trotsky's brandy.
(TOM takes it, drinks.)

TOM: Mmmm. I'll drink it, even if I don't believe it.

VIRGINIA: Isn't it fabulous? Now a cigar.

TOM: No cigar, thanks.

VIRGINIA: *(Goes to humidor)* Oh you've got to have one of these.

(Returns with cigar)

Guess who sent her these?

TOM: Can't imagine. Churchill?

VIRGINIA: No. She and Churchill didn't get along. They disagreed about the Italian campaign.

TOM: Uh huh.

VIRGINIA: No actually, Freud sent her these cigars.

Tom: *(Laughing)* Come off it.

VIRGINIA: *(Unwrapping cigar, lighting it for him)* Sigmund Freud sent her these cigars. *Ask* her, if you don't believe me. He wanted to psychoanalyze her, but she said let sleeping dogs lie, and he sent her these cigars just the same. Now enjoy it, for heaven's sake.

*(*TOM *takes the cigar)*

There. Is that fabulous? Or not?

TOM: *(Puffing)* It's fabulous. Everything seems fabulous tonight. It's like walking into one of those storybooks where the pictures pop up. This, the brandy, the dinner, the studio . . . *(HE looks at her.)* You.

VIRGINIA: Me?

TOM: You.

(HE sits down beside her on the couch.)

You're fabulous, too.

VIRGINIA: Thank you very much.

TOM: I mean it. There's been a kind of glow around you all evening.

VIRGINIA: A glow?

TOM: A golden glow.

VIRGINIA: Oh phooey. That's because you haven't seen enough of your Brontë woman.

TOM: Maybe. *(Pause)* Or maybe not.

VIRGINIA: Well it's certainly been a long time since I've seen a man.

TOM: You seem to have survived pretty well without one.

VIRGINIA: Just lately. I used to be obsessed with men.

TOM: You?

VIRGINIA: Oh sure. Even when I was eight, I ran away with the gardener's son out in Long Island. We got as far as the gatehouse.

TOM: Big deal.

VIRGINIA: And I've been married twice.

TOM: Married?

VIRGINIA: Twice. I swear. The first was an Englishman. Gram had thrown me into this girls' boarding school in Switzerland, and he started hanging around, and I thought, my God, what's this? Something that doesn't giggle and borrow my bra. So I left school and married him. Trouble was, he started giggling and borrowing my bra.

TOM: Oh Jesus.

VIRGINIA: So Gram sent him a huge check, which is what he wanted all along, and that ended that.

TOM: One down, one to go.

VIRGINIA: Number two was a truck driver.

TOM: Come on.

VIRGINIA: Number two drove trucks. I came back here, and Gram got me a job in the Metropolitan Museum, cataloguing Greek art in the cellar. One day this man delivered a crate. We opened it up. It was a second-rate copy of the "Discus Thrower." I looked at the statue, and looked at the man, and went off with the real thing.

TOM: To Greece?

VIRGINIA: No, no. To a split-level in the suburbs of Toledo. And he'd be gone days at a time. So I'd sneak a tad of sherry into my morning coffee and when he came back, I wasn't in much shape to defrost his chicken pot pies. So he'd throw them at me.

TOM: The discus thrower . . .

VIRGINIA: I'll say. The real thing can *hurt* . . . So Gram sent *him* a check, and a few more to the various institutions which tried to dry me out, and a few more after that to the psychiatrists who finally gave up and sent me back here to her.

TOM: Oh boy, oh boy.

VIRGINIA: You can see why Gram needs money. I've been kind of expensive, over the years. *(Pause)* Have some more brandy.

(HE gets some.)

TOM: But you're O.K. now, I hope.

VIRGINIA: Oh I don't know. I'm so dependent on other things: Men. Liquor. My grandmother. I wish I could be . . .

TOM: What?

VIRGINIA: Free. *(Pause)* Once Gram wrote a letter to Jung about me.

TOM: *(Ironically)* Why not the best?

VIRGINIA: Exactly. And Jung wrote back that I had a Rapunzel complex.

TOM: Which means . . . ?

VIRGINIA: Oh gosh. Let's see. How does it go? I'm the princess in the enchanted tower, guarded by the old crone, and I'm waiting for some prince to climb up and carry me off in all directions.

TOM: Ah.

VIRGINIA: Even now, that's what he'd say I'm doing. I'm letting down my hair. So you have something to hold onto when you climb up and set me free.

TOM: Do you think that's true? *(Pause)*

VIRGINIA: It's hard to know what's true. And what isn't.

TOM: So I'm discovering . . . What does your grandmother think?

VIRGINIA: Oh she got mad at the old crone part and refused to pay the bill.

TOM: *(Laughing; sets drink down)* Well I'd better get going.

VIRGINIA: Why?

TOM: Otherwise, I'd kiss you.

VIRGINIA: What's wrong with that?

TOM: Nothing. Except that it wouldn't stop there. Before long, the prince would be begging the princess to go to bed with him.

VIRGINIA: No harm in asking.

TOM: I *can't*, Virginia.

VIRGINIA: Because of your wife?

TOM: Because of your grandmother. In her *house*? After all she's *done*?

VIRGINIA: That's why she's done it. *(Pause)*

TOM: Say that again.

VIRGINIA: She wants you to.

TOM: Why?

VIRGINIA: She thinks it's important. She says when you've fallen off a horse, sooner or later you've got to get back into the saddle. *(Pause)*

TOM: Hmmm.

VIRGINIA: You see?

TOM: I see.

VIRGINIA: It's as simple as that.

TOM: And I'm the horse, eh?

VIRGINIA: Oh well . . .

TOM: Not the prince, just the horse.

VIRGINIA: Your cigar's gone out. Here.
(SHE lights a match for his cigar.)

TOM: *(Refusing the light)* Kind of puts a man under the gun, doesn't it? Being told he's a horse.

VIRGINIA: It's just a metaphor.

TOM: Maybe she thinks I'm some sort of stud. Which I'm not.

VIRGINIA: Of course you're not. *Literally.*

TOM: I mean, is that why she wanted to pay the bill? Just for that? Do I get a tip if I'm good? Is she waiting to give me a carrot?

VIRGINIA: She's not waiting. She's sound asleep.

TOM: Well I have to say I'm not that kind of guy.

VIRGINIA: I told her that.

TOM: And what did she say?

VIRGINIA: She said . . . I can't remember what she said.

TOM: Come on, Virginia. What did she say?

(ISABEL *enters through the curtains in exotic black lounging pajamas.*)

ISABEL: I said they're all the same.

TOM: Men? Or horses?

ISABEL: Both.

VIRGINIA: Gram, you're supposed to be asleep.

ISABEL: I'm looking for my book.

VIRGINIA: Please go to bed, Gram.

ISABEL: I can't. I got too involved in the ballgame. Reggie Jackson hit his second home run in the bottom of the tenth, and now I need my book to put me to sleep.

(SHE *looks around.*)

TOM: So you think men are like horses, Mrs. Hoyt.

VIRGINIA: Don't, Tom.

ISABEL: Oh absolutely. And I think every women should know how to ride.

TOM: Did you?

ISABEL: Of course. Side-saddle. On a great, golden gelding.

TOM: And you taught Virginia?

ISABEL: Everything she knows.

TOM: What did you tell her to do when the horse balks, Mrs. Hoyt? Isn't that what horses do occasionally? Don't they balk?

ISABEL: They most certainly do. You can be cantering toward a fence, and they simple refuse. They won't go over.

TOM: And what do you do then?

ISABEL: You show him who's boss. You use a switch. If you have one.

TOM: And if you don't have one?

VIRGINIA: I can't stand this.

(SHE *walks away.*)

ISABEL: *(To TOM)* You turn him around, squeeze with your knees, and try again.

VIRGINIA: Could we change the subject, please?

TOM: *(Pressing home)* What if he still won't do it, Mrs. Hoyt? What if he's not some overbred English gelding you can put through his paces? What if he's a proud American mustang, fresh from the prairies, and not yet ready to be broken in!

ISABEL: Ah, then you simply distract him.

TOM: How?

ISABEL: Give the gentleman more brandy, Virginia.

TOM: No thank you.

ISABEL: *(Crossing to victrola)* Now in my day, whenever we got into trouble . . . (SHE *fusses with victrola.*) Whenever the conversation took a peculiar turn . . . whenever there was some awkwardness in the air . . . why then an orchestra would strike up somewhere . . .

(Music comes up: "Poor Butterfly"★)

And we'd dance . . . Dance with him, Virginia.

VIRGINIA: No thank you, Gram.

ISABEL: Then I'll have to.

(SHE *stands by the victrola, holding out her arms.*)

Well, sir. How long do you intend to remain skulking in the stag line?

(TOM *reluctantly crosses to her.*)

Fitzgerald used to give a little bow. (TOM *does.*) And then we'd dance.

(THEY *dance.*)

Oh, you're wonderful.

★See Special Note on copyright page.

(THEY dance more. SHE does a little spin.)

Come here, I'll show you something that Adele Astaire taught me.

(THEY dance more.)

He's getting good, Virginia. You don't know what you're missing.

VIRGINIA: I'll sit this one out, Gram.

ISABEL: Well then turn it off, quickly, before I start doing a mad, frantic Charleston on top of that table.

(VIRGINIA turns off the music. The dancing stops; ISABEL turns to Tom.)

Well. Have I distracted you?

TOM: *(Panting)* I'll say.

ISABEL: Good. Then I'll go to bed if I can find my book.

VIRGINIA: What were you reading, Gram?

ISABEL: I'm not sure. You see how vague I am? I think it was *The Great Gatsby*. I had just gotten to that long section where Gatsby takes Daisy up to his room, and they spend this marvelous night together. Oh I'm furious. It's by far the best part of the book.

TOM: There's no such section in *Gatsby*, Mrs. Hoyt.

ISABEL: There most certainly is. Fitzgerald gave it to me in manuscript, and I've read it many times. It's superb. Best thing he did. Pulls out all the stops. Look on my desk, Virginia. *(To TOM)* And you, sir. Look on the table hall.

TOM: I will. But there's no such thing in all Fitzgerald.

(HE goes out.)

VIRGINIA: Gram, what are you up to?

ISABEL: *(Quickly; to VIRGINIA)* Get back on your horse.

VIRGINIA: What?

ISABEL: And give him a glimpse of the barn.

VIRGINIA: The barn?

ISABEL: Something he wants! On the other side of the fence! Have you forgotten everything about riding?

(TOM *comes back in.*)

TOM: It's not out there.

ISABEL: *(Whispering; to* VIRGINIA*)* A glimpse of the barn, and he'll go right over.

TOM: I said it's not out there, Mrs. Hoyt.

ISABEL: What isn't?

TOM: Your Fitzgerald.

ISABEL: Was I reading Fitzgerald?

TOM: You said you were.

ISABEL: I must have been dreaming.

TOM: Oh.

ISABEL: Dreaming, reading, it's all the same. Actually, I must have been reading Walter Babcock McCoy. And he's right by my bed, where he belongs.

(SHE *starts out.*)

Goodnight, all.

(SHE *exits through the curtains.*)

VIRGINIA: *(Picking up the empty brandy glass and ashtray)* Well, I'll clean up.

TOM: She's got it, doesn't she?

VIRGINIA: *(As she works)* She certainly does! Now where's that cat?

TOM: No, I mean she's got the lost chapter.

VIRGINIA: Here kitty, kitty, kitty.

TOM: Unless she was teasing.

VIRGINIA: It must be in with her.

TOM: The manuscript.

VIRGINIA: The *cat.* Here kitty, kitty, kitty . . . Well I give up.

(SHE *starts out.*)

TOM: She said Fitzgerald stayed in the studio.

VIRGINIA: I guess he did.

TOM: Did she visit him there?

VIRGINIA: She painted him there.

TOM: Did she sleep with him there?

VIRGINIA: Oh stop.

TOM: She slept with him, and he wrote about it, and she's got what he wrote.

VIRGINIA: You'd better go.

(SHE *starts out.*)

TOM: Wait.

(SHE *stops.*)

Can I at least finish my brandy? *(Pause)*

VIRGINIA: All right.

(SHE *comes back in, pours him another; holds the bottle.*)

TOM: She's sitting on something, isn't she?

VIRGINIA: You think so?

TOM: I know so. She's sitting on something big. *(Pause)* Isn't she? *(Pause)*

VIRGINIA: Yes.

TOM: What's she sitting on?

VIRGINIA: She's sitting on a golden egg, Tom.

TOM: Knew it.

VIRGINIA: That's because you're so smart, Tom. And I hope you're also smart enough to remember what happened when they started messing around with the goose. *(Pause)*

TOM: *(Swirling his brandy)* Have you seen the manuscript?

VIRGINIA: *(Taking a glass)* I'm going to have one of these.

TOM: Don't.

VIRGINIA: Then stop.

TOM: At least tell me if you've seen it. *(Pause)*

VIRGINIA: No.

TOM: Sure you have. Have you read it?

VIRGINIA: No.

TOM: But you've seen it.

VIRGINIA: *(Pouring herself a glass)* One more word, and I drink this, Tom. I swear. *(Pause)*

TOM: All right. I'll stop.

VIRGINIA: Honestly.

TOM: I said I'll stop. *(Long pause; they eye each other.)* Just tell me what it looks like.

VIRGINIA: *(Raising her glass)* I warned you. *(Pause.)*

TOM: That is your choice. (VIRGINIA *looks at him.)* I mean, you wanted to be free . . . You're a human being, after all. *(Pause)* Not a horse. *(Pause)*

VIRGINIA: I know it. *(Pause. SHE takes a good, long defiant slug of the brandy.)*

TOM: *(Trying to stop her)* Oh hey . . . *(Pause)* I just wanted to know what it *looked* like.

VIRGINIA: You tell me.

TOM: Let's see . . . What would it look like? . . . It's an old black loose-leaf notebook . . .

VIRGINIA: That's it.

TOM: Is that what it looks like?

VIRGINIA: Isn't that what all old manuscripts look like? *(SHE pours herself another drink.)*

TOM: An unpublished chapter . . . from *The Great Gatsby.* I knew it!

VIRGINIA: Of course you did.

TOM: It would solve everything. It would make that whole strange book come suddenly clear!

VIRGINIA: Possibly.

TOM: And it would deal with sex. Fitzgerald was a prude about sex. This would be the first and only time he wrote about it!

VIRGINIA: Probably.

TOM: Sure! And can you imagine what he did with it? That glittering prose! Oh Jesus, this is a major find! And—and it means that your grandmother, Isabel Hastings Hoyt, was at least a partial model for Daisy Buchanan, who happens to be the most enticing woman in all American literature!

VIRGINIA: Naturally.

TOM: Of course! Sex! Sex! Sex is the heart of the Golden Age! She said it was Marx, but it's Freud! Oh my God! This is stupendous! And it's all right there, a black book!

VIRGINIA: Obviously. *(Pause. HE looks at her.)*

TOM: What happens to it?

VIRGINIA: Happens?

TOM: After she dies?

VIRGINIA: Oh.

TOM: What happens?

VIRGINIA: *(Carefully)* It would come to me. It would be the one thing I'd get. *(Pause)*

TOM: *(Looking at her)* Daisy Buchanan's granddaughter.

VIRGINIA: *(Curtseying)* How do you do. Of course, she might be pulling your leg.

TOM: Yeah . . .

VIRGINIA: It might not be Fitzgerald at all.

TOM: Hmmm.

VIRGINIA: It might be something else entirely.

TOM: Might be . . .

VIRGINIA: It might be an old story, for example. By Henry James. Or it might be a play.

TOM: A play . . .

VIRGINIA: By Shaw. Or Philip Barry. Or Eugene O'Neill. Or it might be just an old melodrama, by Walter Babcock McCoy.

TOM: You mean she might be playing games.

VIRGINIA: Might be.

TOM: Just fooling around.

VIRGINIA: Might be.

TOM: Maybe she got the idea from me, and is just using it to egg me on.

VIRGINIA: Maybe.

TOM: But why?

VIRGINIA: Oh that's easy. Because you're so attractive, Tom.

She's pretending you're Gatsby, and I'm Daisy, and she's doing everything she can to repeat the past.

TOM: Well you tell her, please, that some critics say Gatsby never sleeps with Daisy. He was too honorable a man.

VIRGINIA: That's fascinating. Goodnight.

(SHE *starts turning off the lights.*)

TOM: Anyway, I can't imagine your grandmother shacking up with Fitzgerald.

VIRGINIA: Oh I can. I'm sure she was very discreet about it. She probably fortified herself with a drink or two. And waited till everything was pitch dark. But then I can see her tip-toeing upstairs to the studio, and slipping into his bed. If she were asked. Here kitty, kitty, kitty.

TOM: *(Carefully)* I think the cat might be up in the studio.

VIRGINIA: You really think so?

TOM: I really do.

(HE *looks at her, goes on up the stairs. SHE turns out the last of the lights, as we black out. In the darkness, over the speakers, we hear the sound of the last chorus of the last aria in* Aida: *"O Terra Adio."*★ *The lights come up slowly.* ISABEL *sits in her chair, in her shawl, listening to the opera from an old Capehart radio-victrola. After a moment,* VIRGINIA *and* TOM *appear in the doorway,* L. *They wear informal clothes. They watch her. Then* TOM *goes on upstairs.* VIRGINIA *remains. SHE holds a blue piece of note paper. SHE watches her grandmother fondly, then comes into the room.*)

VIRGINIA: You wanted to see me, Gram?

ISABEL: *(Holding up her hand)* Ssshh.

(SHE *speaks the final words of Amneris along with the singer.*) "Pace . . . Pace . . . Pace t'imploro . . . Pace . . . Pace . . ." (We *hear applause and an announcer's voice from the radio.*)

ANNOUNCER'S VOICE: And the golden curtain descends on the final act of Aida . . .

★See Special Note on copyright page.

ISABEL: *(Joining him) Aida,* by Giuseppi Verdi.
(SHE *gestures for Virginia to turn off the radio.)*
The Met's last broadcast.

VIRGINIA: *(Fixing her pillows)* Oh they're already on tour, Gram. They'll be back next fall.

ISABEL: I won't.

VIRGINIA: Stop it, Gram.

ISABEL: Yes, well, that rich, deep, contralto voice was the Princess Amneris, sealing herself up in a tomb, so Aida, her slave girl, can go free.

VIRGINIA: That's not quite it, Gram.

ISABEL: What do you mean?

VIRGINIA: Aida joins her lover in the tomb. And Amneris goes free.

ISABEL: Are you sure?

VIRGINIA I think so.

ISABEL: Of course Verdi wrote it when he was very old. He must have been losing his grip. Much as I adore Verdi. I met him, you know.

VIRGINIA: You didn't meet Verdi, Gram.

ISABEL: I most certainly did. I was travelling through Parma with my mother, and we met this nice old man with a beard who kissed me on the top of my head. That was Verdi. I'm practically positive. Unless it was Michelangelo.

VIRGINIA: *(Hugging her)* Oh, Gram. I love you . . .

ISABEL: You should listen to Verdi. He wrote operas about liberation. Even his name meant freedom. They'd write it on walls.

VIRGINIA: *(Indicating blue piece of paper)* You left this note on the stairs, Gram. (SHE *reads.)* "Please stop by."

ISABEL: Oh yes. You're so popular now, I have to waylay you.

VIRGINIA: Now, Gram.

ISABEL: Well you are. Come, sit down beside me. You're the belle of the ball. You should hire a social secretary.

VIRGINIA: We were taking a walk, Gram. It's a lovely day.

ISABEL: I'm glad you're getting out.

VIRGINIA: So am I.

ISABEL: Now see that he takes you around.

VIRGINIA: Around?

ISABEL: Shows you off. Introduces you to his friends. Soon you'll be having a perfectly marvelous time.

VIRGINIA: I *am* having a marvelous time, Gram.

ISABEL: Oh I know you are. But it would be even more marvelous if you met more people.

VIRGINIA: Oh well.

ISABEL: No, really. Take him out of the paddock and onto the trail.

VIRGINIA: He's not a horse, Gram.

ISABEL: Well he doesn't seem to be a writer. I have not heard the typewriter banging away recently. That's not what I've heard banging away.

VIRGINIA: He's hit a snag, Gram.

ISABEL: Of course he has. He's met you. He's been distracted from his labors by a beautiful woman. Why don't you put him back to work?

VIRGINIA: I can't just—

ISABEL: Of course you can. I had to do the same thing with Picasso. We had a hell of a row, but he took it right in stride, and afterwards he painted the "Guernica."

VIRGINIA: Oh, Gram . . .

ISABEL: No, I'm serious. Go meet more men. And when you're shaking hands, and saying goodbye, say it very softly, so they have to lean over to hear you. Then they'll know that you're free and clear for the summer season.

VIRGINIA: I don't care about being free and clear for the summer season.

ISABEL: Well you should. And you should send this one back to his book, so you'll have money to enjoy it.

VIRGINIA: Oh Gram, why did you encourage us, if you're breaking it up?

ISABEL: I thought it would do you good.

VIRGINIA: It has. I haven't had a drink in weeks.

ISABEL: Fine. That means it took.

VIRGINIA: Took?

ISABEL: Like a vaccination, dear. A touch of the serum, so you don't get the real disease. Oh it might hurt a little, it might itch, but that only means it took, my love. It makes you immune.

VIRGINIA: I don't want to be immune.

ISABEL: Of course you do. What is a woman unless she's free? And how can she be free if she's tied to one man?

VIRGINIA: That's your philosophy, Gram.

ISABEL: It most certainly is. I've had eighty years to work it out.

VIRGINIA: Well it's not mine.

ISABEL: Well it ought to be, by now.

VIRGINIA: Well it isn't. I'm a different generation, Gram. I have my own ideas. I think . . . I think . . . I think I love him, Gram.

ISABEL: That's an insidious word.

VIRGINIA: Not to me.

ISABEL: Well it is to me. I've learned to distrust it completely.

VIRGINIA: I haven't.

ISABEL: Then it's time you did. It seems to me we've heard that song before.

VIRGINIA: I know . . .

ISABEL: It seems to me the orchestra played that particular tune in Switzerland. And Toledo. And various other spots in the free world.

VIRGINIA: But this is different.

ISABEL: It certainly is. This one is younger than you are.

VIRGINIA: Nobody cares about that any more, Gram. Not if you're in love.

ISABEL: Is he? Has he said so?

VIRGINIA: No. But there's something between us, Gram. Something special. I can tell.

ISABEL: You don't think it's something to do with me?

VIRGINIA: No.

ISABEL: You don't think he sees you as a way to get to me?

VIRGINIA: No!

ISABEL: Does he ask about me?

VIRGINIA: Sometimes.

ISABEL: What do you tell him?

VIRGINIA: I tell him what I know.

ISABEL: Does he talk about the black book?

VIRGINIA: No.

ISABEL: Virginia . . .

VIRGINIA: Once in a while.

ISABEL: What do you tell him?

VIRGINIA: I tell him not to talk about it.

ISABEL: Why don't you tell him there isn't one?

VIRGINIA: Oh, Gram . . .

ISABEL: Why don't you?

VIRGINIA: Because I don't dare.

ISABEL: Sweetheart, I *know* this man. I've met him before. He comes out of the West, all energy and charm, and he's wonderful to go around with for a while. But he's hungry, my love. He wants more than you or I could ever give him. He could break your heart.

VIRGINIA: I don't care. I'm not you, Gram. I'm different. And I need him.

ISABEL: *(With a sigh)* Oh dear. Then we might have to change course.

VIRGINIA: What will you do?

ISABEL: Sound him out.

VIRGINIA: How?

ISABEL: I'll talk to him.

VIRGINIA: Talk to him?

ISABEL: Just talk. *(Pause)*

VIRGINIA: All right.

ISABEL: Would you get him, please?

VIRGINIA: Now?

ISABEL: Why not now?

VIRGINIA: He's got a class on Monday. He has to prepare.

ISABEL: So do I. Send him down. *(Pause)*

VIRGINIA: All right.

    (SHE goes to the hallway and calls.)
    Tom!

ISABEL: *(To herself)* Tom, Tom, the piper's son . . .

TOM'S VOICE: Yo?

VIRGINIA: Gram wants to see you.

TOM'S VOICE: Be right down.

VIRGINIA: He's coming down, Gram.

ISABEL: I'll bet he is. Why don't you go make tea?

VIRGINIA: I want to be here, Gram.

ISABEL: Make tea. No tea bags, either. Give it time. Let it
    steep.

VIRGINIA: I'm staying here, Gram.

ISABEL: And why is that?

VIRGINIA: So you won't bully him, Gram.

ISABEL: I see.

VIRGINIA: Oh please, Gram. Don't ruin it, please! I don't
    care why he's here, or what he wants. Just let him last a
    little longer. I'm so scared of being left alone!

ISABEL: And are you scared, if you make tea, of being left
    alone with the sherry?

VIRGINIA: I'll make tea, Gram. I'll make the best tea you
    ever had.

    *(SHE turns to go out as TOM appears in the door, carrying the
    cat. HE is in his shirt-sleeves.)*

TOM: *(To VIRGINIA)* Our friend seems to want to go out.

VIRGINIA: I'll take her.

    (SHE takes the cat from TOM, and hurries off downstairs.)

TOM: *(To ISABEL; coming into the room)* Great cat.

ISABEL: I don't have time to discuss cats. *(Indicating chair)* Pull up your chair. Let's lay our cards on the table, you and I.

TOM: Fair enough.

ISABEL: Not so long ago, I told you some of my deepest feelings. Do you remember?

TOM: Yes.

ISABEL: Well now I'd like you to tell me yours. About my granddaughter. *(Pause)*

TOM: Ah.

ISABEL: Yes. Ah.

TOM: I like her.

ISABEL: How much?

TOM: A lot.

ISABEL: Do you love her?

TOM: I've only known her a couple of months.

ISABEL: She says she loves you.

TOM: Well I . . . don't know, Mrs. Hoyt.

ISABEL: You'd know if you loved her.

TOM: I'll tell you this: every time I'm with her, I like her more.

ISABEL: More than your wife, shivering in Minnesota? More than that poor creature, wandering around the moors, teaching the Brontës?

TOM: Your granddaughter's different.

ISABEL: I'll say she is.

TOM: She's special. There's something about her . . .

ISABEL: There certainly is. *(Pause)* All right, now, be quiet, because I'm changing my mind. Which at my age is very difficult to do.

(SHE thinks. HE watches her.)

There. I've changed it.

TOM: You have?

ISABEL: Yes. I've come to a decision. I've decided to let you marry my granddaughter.

TOM: Marry her?

ISABEL: That's what I've decided. She seems to be instinctively monogamous, like a mallard duck, or I suppose I should say a swan.

TOM: Mrs. Hoyt . . .

ISABEL: Now as you know, I'm not particularly fond of marriage. But I have known several people who liked it. The Lunts, for example, absolutely swore by it, and in times of trouble, we might as well look to the Lunts. So what I have decided is that you should marry my granddaughter, and live with us here, and support her by finishing that book. *(Pause)* You may reply.

TOM: I'm still married, Mrs. Hoyt.

ISABEL: I know you are. Technically. But nowadays I hear you can order a divorce over the telephone.

TOM: I'm not ready to get married again.

ISABEL: Of course you're not. Neither am I. But apparently she is. And so we've got to be good sports about it.

TOM: Mrs. Hoyt, please—

ISABEL: No, no. Now listen. I've thought it through. It'll be fun actually. You can have the run of the house. You can chase each other around in your pajamas, which I used to do with Bertrand Russell. We'll be aggressively domestic. We'll have meals together! We'll eat leftovers and talk about laundry! Oh I can't wait! You can teach in the morning, and write our book in the afternoon, and we'll all live happily ever after.

TOM: Does she know about this?

ISABEL: Of course not. Good heavens. But I know she wants it. I'm sure of that.

TOM: Mrs. Hoyt. I'm extremely fond of your granddaughter, but I can't marry her. I've already made a mess of marriage. I'm sorry, but the answer is no.

ISABEL: This reminds me of the secret negotiations after World War One. I was there, you know.

TOM: You were at Versailles?

ISABEL: Oh yes. They had to decide what to do with the Ottoman Empire. We called it talking Turkey.

TOM: *(Shaking his head)* Talking Turkey . . .

ISABEL: Oh yes. And I'll tell you all about it if you marry my granddaughter.

TOM: Mrs. Hoyt, I swear to you here and now, I'll do everything I can to take care of your granddaughter.

ISABEL: Take care of her?

TOM: That I swear.

ISABEL: You mean make her your mistress?

TOM: I mean take care of her. She'll be my friend. *(Pause)*

ISABEL: Well then, I want you to ease her into the world. Find her a job. Where you teach, maybe. In the library. *Something.*

TOM: Sure.

ISABEL: And finish that *book.*

TOM: I'll try, Mrs. Hoyt.

ISABEL: You see there isn't much money, and she'll be all alone, and I'm terribly concerned how she'll survive.

TOM: *(Touching her hand)* I'll do my best, Mrs. Hoyt. I promise.

ISABEL: Thank you. And because you said that, I want to give you something.

TOM: Give me something?

ISABEL: I'll give you something right now. Please go to my desk.

TOM: All right.
    (HE does.)

ISABEL: And look in the right drawer . . .

TOM: Right drawer . . . All right.
    (HE does.)

ISABEL: And see if you can find my checkbook and my fountain pen.

TOM: Your checkbook?

ISABEL: I want to give you a check. It won't be much. But it will help you to tide her over.

TOM: You're talking about money.

ISABEL: What else is there to talk about at this point?

TOM: Something profoundly important to American culture.

ISABEL: Sounds like money to me.

TOM: I'm talking about the black book, Mrs. Hoyt.

ISABEL: Oh that.

TOM: Yes that. Give me that, Mrs. Hoyt, and let me publish it, and your granddaughter would be set up for life.

ISABEL: I said I was dreaming. Don't you remember?

TOM: I don't think you were.

ISABEL: Then I made it up. It was just something to keep you around. I'm sorry. That was naughty. I apologize.

TOM: I don't believe that either.

ISABEL: All right. What if I have what you say I have?

TOM: I know you do.

ISABEL: And what if I don't want it published?

TOM: Then of course we'd wait.

ISABEL: Until what?

TOM: Your . . . demise.

ISABEL: You mean when I kick the bucket?

TOM: All right. Yes.

ISABEL: What if I still don't want.

TOM: Oh Mrs. Hoyt . . .

ISABEL: Don't you think, dear man, there are some things in this world better left unsaid? Suppose Scott Fitzgerald thought that. Suppose I think so too.

TOM: Suppose you're wrong. Standards change. Suppose Fitzgerald would be proud to have it published now.

ISABEL: And who decides?

TOM: Me. Let me. Oh come on, Mrs. Hoyt, please. You've got a momentous piece of literature waiting in the wings. You've got America's finest writer, in his finest work, bringing it all together for the first

and last time! You've got the heart of the matter in
that book, Mrs. Hoyt. The absolute center of the
Golden Age. Let me just look at it! Let me just see!
(Pause)

ISABEL: I'm suddenly very tired.

TOM: Then let's talk about it tomorrow.

ISABEL: Not tomorrow.

TOM: Name the time then.

ISABEL: Never.

TOM: Never?

ISABEL: Never again.

TOM: Then what do I do?

ISABEL: Love her, if you can. Care for her. Make her happy.
And I promise that one day she'll bring you whatever she
gets from me.

TOM: You mean . . . wait.

ISABEL: That's it.

TOM: Just wait.

ISABEL: And hope. And be a good boy.

TOM: No.

ISABEL: No?

TOM: Let me propose another deal . . . Suppose I leave.
Take a break. Take a breather.

ISABEL: Where would you go?

TOM: Home, maybe. Back to Minnesota.

ISABEL: To your wife?

TOM: To my roots.

ISABEL: Oh I knew it.

TOM: It's hard to hang around if I'm not trusted.

ISABEL: *She* trusts you.

TOM: You don't.

ISABEL: You'd shatter her!

TOM: She always has you.

ISABEL: Not always, sir.

TOM: Then show me the book.

ISABEL: *(Drawing herself up)* There are certain expressions which I hear have wormed their way onto the stage. I'll use one now. You are a *shit*, sir!

TOM: Oh no.

ISABEL: Oh yes. You are blackmailing me!

TOM: Blackmail . . . Who's blackmailing who around here? Oh boy, I've found the Golden Age, all right! Right here in this room! You've got lists, games, manipulations! Hell, what am I? Just another slave? Just another flunky you've brought around the house to fix the plumbing!

ISABEL: *(Pointing to the door)* Get out.

TOM: Gladly! *(HE starts for the door.)*

ISABEL: Wait.

(HE stops; SHE leans on chair.)

Before you do, I have to ask you to do me one more favor.

TOM: What is it?

ISABEL: Call the doctor. His number is by the telephone in the hall.

(SHE almost collapses. TOM comes to help her, calling "Virginia! Virginia!" The lights go to black. Almost immediately the lights come up again. It is late at night. A couple of lights are on in the room, and another in the hall. VIRGINIA comes out from Isabel's room. TOM leans on the hall door jamb. They look at each other.)

TOM: How is she?

VIRGINIA: Fine. Perfectly fine.

TOM: I just got rid of the doctor.

VIRGINIA: She hates doctors.

TOM: He thinks she should go to the hospital.

VIRGINIA: That's why she hates them.

TOM: Well he thinks she should.

VIRGINIA: Well she won't. And I don't blame her. She'd last about a week.

(SHE starts to break down. HE makes a move toward her. SHE holds up her hand.)

I'm perfectly fine.

(SHE glances toward brandy, glances away.) And so is she. She's sound alseep. He gave her a pill.

TOM: You should go to bed yourself.

VIRGINIA: I will. I plan to. *(Pause)* Where's the cat?

TOM I have no idea.

VIRGINIA: I haven't seen it in ages.

TOM: *(Putting an arm around her)* Ssshh. It'll turn up.

VIRGINIA: What did you say to her?

TOM: Me?

VIRGINIA: What did you *say?*

TOM: I simply said . . .

VIRGINIA: You asked for the black book, didn't you?

TOM: I asked to see it, yes.

VIRGINIA: Why?

TOM: It just came up.

VIRGINIA: You promised never to mention it.

TOM: It just came *up*. And hell, why not? I mean, is it a crime to love literature around here? Is it a major crime to want to preserve the past? *(Pause)*

VIRGINIA: She wants you out of the house.

TOM: I'm all packed.

VIRGINIA: She never wants to see you again.

TOM: Ditto.

VIRGINIA: I had to beg her to let you stay even tonight.

TOM: I'm only staying because of you. Tomorrow I'm off. Oh boy, and glad to go. I'm ready for some good fresh air. *(Pause)* You should be, too.

VIRGINIA: Me?

TOM: I hope you'll get out, too.

VIRGINIA: Oh well.

TOM: I'm serious. I hope we can still see each other. In the real world.

VIRGINIA: She said you were going home.

TOM: I'm not sure I can.

VIRGINIA: Because of her?

TOM: Because of you.

VIRGINIA: Oh stop.

TOM: I just got all riled up over a few pieces of paper which probably don't exist anyway.

VIRGINIA: You don't care about that any more?

TOM: I couldn't care less. I swear. I care about you. *(Pause)*

VIRGINIA: She made me get it out.

TOM: What?

VIRGINIA: She made me put it into her hands. She wanted to hold it.

TOM: Well it's important to her, at least.

VIRGINIA: Oh yes. She wouldn't let go. Finally she got so sleepy I could take it away.

TOM: Well, keep an eye on it. It might be your meal ticket some day.

VIRGINIA: No.

TOM: No?

VIRGINIA: She wants me to burn it.

TOM: *Burn* it?

VIRGINIA: Tomorrow morning. When she wakes up. I'm to burn it in her fireplace, systematically, page by page, right in front of her eyes.

TOM: *Why?*

VIRGINIA: Because she doesn't want you to get your hands on it.

TOM: Oh my lord.

VIRGINIA: She thinks that's all you care about.

TOM: Yeah well you tell her from me that I'm through with Fitzgerald and old manuscripts and literature in general. I plan to go back to graduate school and get a degree in computer science! It makes no never mind to me whether she burns it, or uses it for scratch paper for her goddam lists, or—you won't do it, will you?

VIRGINIA: Do what?

TOM: Burn it.

VIRGINIA: I'll have to.

TOM: She'll change her mind in the morning.

VIRGINIA: I don't think so.

TOM: Then persuade her.

VIRGINIA: Why?

TOM: So you can have it.

VIRGINIA: I don't want it.

TOM: But you'll need it.

VIRGINIA: Oh I don't know, Tom. Maybe I'd be better off without it.

TOM: Oh Jesus.

VIRGINIA: I mean it's caused nothing but trouble.

TOM: You're right. You're absolutely right. It's stood between us from the word go. It. It. It. Seems all we talk about is IT . . . Where is it, by the way?

VIRGINIA: What?

TOM: Maybe you should go get it.

VIRGINIA: I will not.

TOM: Maybe we should look at it.

VIRGINIA: Tom!

TOM: While she's asleep.

VIRGINIA: Are you out of your mind?

TOM: Just to get it out of our systems.

VIRGINIA: Oh please.

TOM: I think she wants us to.

VIRGINIA: She does not!

TOM: Subconsciously. That's why she got it out. So we could look at it. That's what her buddy Freud would say.

VIRGINIA: I think you're wrong.

TOM: Let me just glance at it. Before it goes.

VIRGINIA: I said NO, Tom. No. Period.

TOM: Oh God in heaven! What do I do?

VIRGINIA: Maybe you should just go to bed, Tom.

TOM: Go to *bed?* With that about to be *burned?* Virgil would have burned the *Aeneid* if they hadn't stopped him! Byron's wife burned his *diaries* because no one intervened! And you sit there and tell me to go to bed.

VIRGINIA: All I know is I'm exhausted. *(Pause)*

TOM: You're right. Forgive me. Come on. We'll go to bed.

VIRGINIA: I'm not coming up, Tom.

TOM: What?

VIRGINIA: I'm not coming up.

TOM: Why not?

VIRGINIA: I don't want to.

TOM: One last time. In the studio.

VIRGINIA: No.

TOM: I'll come to your room then.

VIRGINIA: I won't be there, Tom.

TOM: Won't be there?

VIRGINIA: I'm sleeping on the couch back in her dressing room.

TOM: Why?

VIRGINIA: Because she asked me to.

TOM: WHY?

VIRGINIA: Maybe she thinks you'll steal it, Tom.

TOM: She said that?

VIRGINIA: She said lots of things.

TOM: And what did you say? *(Pause)* Did you say I wouldn't?

VIRGINIA: No.

TOM: Good God, Virginia! Who do you think I *am?*

VIRGINIA: I don't know.

(TOM stares at her, then turns and storms out of the room and up the stairs. VIRGINIA stands up, looks after him, turns off the lights by a main switch, next to the curtains, and goes in, slowly. The only light in the main room now comes from the hall and through the window. After a moment, we hear TOM angrily coming down the stairs. HE carries a stuffed laundry bag, and a suitcase. As HE passes the doorway, HE calls into the room:)

TOM: I'll get the rest of my stuff in the morning!

(HE *continues angrily with his stuff out of sight beyond the door. Another moment. Then HE reappears at the doorway. More quietly.*)

I said, goodbye. (HE *looks in to the room.*) Virginia?

(HE *stands in the doorway for a moment. Then HE takes a step into the room. HE calls quietly towards Isabel's room.*) Virginia.

(*No answer. HE looks around the room, comes in a little further. HE looks towards Isabel's room, starts for it. His shoes make a noise. HE sits on a chair and carefully takes off his shoes. HE moves quietly, threading his way through the furniture to Isabel's doorway. HE pauses near the doorway, unable to make up his mind. Then HE slips quietly in. A long moment. Then HE reappears stealthily. A large, black, worn loose-leaf notebook tied with ribbons is now in his hands. Slowly, HE makes his way toward the hallway, L. HE stumbles over something, says, "Damn cat." HE gets to the hall. HE puts the book very carefully on a table by the hall. HE finds a match, lights it, begins to untie the ribbons. Suddenly all the lights in the room go on, full blaze. ISABEL stands framed in her doorway, one hand on the lightswitch, the other holding a small shotgun. SHE wears a long white nightgown, and she looks wildly spectacular.*)

ISABEL: (*Pointing the gun at him; hissing*) Leave. That. Alone.

TOM: Mrs. Hoyt . . .

ISABEL: Leave it *alone*.

TOM: (*Indicating camera*) I was only—

ISABEL: Take off your clothes.

TOM: What?

ISABEL: Take off your clothes or I'll blow your head off!

TOM: (*Half laughing*) I'm not going to—

ISABEL: (*Aiming the gun*) I could bring down a bird at fifty yards.

(TOM *hurriedly starts unbuttoning his shirt.*)

TOM: Why do I have to—

ISABEL: *(Grimly)* Do it!

(TOM gets his shirt off. VIRGINIA comes hurriedly out from within, wrapping a bathrobe around herself.)

VIRGINIA: Gram!

ISABEL: *(Hardly noticing her; grimly, to TOM)* Now your trousers, sir.

TOM: *(Pleadingly, to VIRGINIA)* She wants me to—

ISABEL: Take off your *trousers!*

VIRGINIA: Gram . . .

ISABEL: I said, your *trousers!*

(TOM hurriedly takes off his pants. HE stands there in his shorts. To VIRGINIA)

Shall we leave him a fig leaf?

VIRGINIA: Oh yes, Gram!

ISABEL: *(To TOM)* Would you have left *me* one?

TOM: *(Helplessly)* I just wanted to see.

ISABEL: Well so do I! *(SHE gestures with her gun; TOM is about to remove his undershorts.)*

VIRGINIA: *(Stepping between them)* Oh, Gram, what are you doing?

ISABEL: I'm leaving you a picture. There it is. Portrait of a man. Do you want it? Is it worth it? Remember: he can steal your very soul!

(SHE lowers the gun. TOM grabs his clothes and rushes from the room. ISABEL leans the gun somewhere and crosses to the table where he has left the manuscript. VIRGINIA stands amazed. ISABEL gathers up the manuscript and clutches it to her chest. SHE starts back for her room, then turns and looks at VIRGINIA, swaying forward.)

Help me, Virginia.

(VIRGINIA rushes to her as ISABEL lurches forward. VIRGINIA catches her in her arms as the papers scatter at her feet. Blackout. A moment. Then a radio announcer's voice is heard over the speakers:)

RADIO ANNOUNCER'S VOICE: . . . Also in the local news: America reached the end of an era last night when Mrs. Isabel Hastings Hoyt, a prominent figure in New York society during the period after World War I, died in her sleep at her home on East 81st Street. A recluse in recent years, Mrs. Hoyt is said to have been at one time the friend and confidante of many of the important artists and writers of her day. Her handsome brownstone house, with its rooms of fine furniture, will be purchased in its entirety by the National Historical Association. Mrs. Hoyt is survived by a single granddaughter, who served as her companion and was with her when she died.

(The lights come slowly up in the room. It looks just the same. From the window, once again, comes the sense of late afternoon. A suitcase is near the hall. The curtains are fully open now, and we can see partly into Isabel's room. We see the end of her bed, stripped of its covers. The doorbell rings. VIRGINIA enters, from her grandmother's room, in a dark dress. The doorknocker is heard. SHE stands, does nothing. Then we hear a key working in a lock. Then TOM's voice is heard, off and below.)

TOM'S VOICE: Virginia!

(SHE hides the manuscript behind a pillow on the couch. After a moment, TOM comes in.)

TOM: *(Holding up a key)* I still have a key.

VIRGINIA: Just put it on the table.

(HE does. Pause)

I've been nervous about the door. The lawyers said not even to answer it. The worst sort of people read the obituaries.

TOM: So I've heard.

VIRGINIA: There's even a security guard. Prowling around somewhere out there. To protect the loot.

TOM: I met him. I told him I was a friend of the family.

(Pause)

VIRGINIA: Some friend. You weren't even here.

TOM: I just got your message.

VIRGINIA: I left messages all over.

TOM: I didn't know.

VIRGINIA: It was in the *Times*.

TOM: I was out of town.

VIRGINIA: There was even a picture.

TOM: I was away.

VIRGINIA: I gave them the one from the old *Life*. Waving goodbye. I thought at least that would bring you around.

TOM: I was in Saint Paul. For the whole month. *(Pause)*

VIRGINIA: Oh. *(Pause)*

TOM: But it didn't work. I came back to see you. *(Pause)*

VIRGINIA: You see, there was so much to do. You don't realize till it happens. I mean the medical certificate, and the funeral men, and the lawyers, and the bank, and the newspapers.

TOM: I'm very sorry.

VIRGINIA: Well I managed. Somehow. Amazingly enough. *(Pause)* And of course Gram left a list.

(HE steps toward her.)

I'm all right. I'm fine.

TOM: Look. Hey. I'm sorry about that night.

VIRGINIA: That was a terrible thing you did.

TOM: I got carried away.

VIRGINIA: You both did terrible things.

TOM: I didn't want it burned.

VIRGINIA: She did.

TOM: I know. I'm sorry. Really. I feel like hell. *(Pause)*

VIRGINIA: Would you like a drink?

TOM: No thanks.

VIRGINIA: It's right there. The brandy. I haven't touched it. I'm over that, too, I hope. Take it. Before the historians get into it.

TOM: No thanks. *(Pause)*

VIRGINIA: I have to be out of here today.

TOM: Where will you go?

VIRGINIA: I'm not sure. There's this hotel for women.

TOM: Oh Christ.

VIRGINIA: I know it. *(Pause)*

TOM: And then what?

VIRGINIA: Oh. Gram left another list. Want to hear?

TOM: Sure

VIRGINIA: *(Takes a blue piece of paper out of her purse)* There's no date so I don't know when she wrote it. *(Puts on glasses, reads)* "Prospects for Virginia." *(Pause)* "Make hors d'oeuvres for parties." *(Pause)* "Take care of cats when people go away." *(Pause)* "Find a girls' boarding school, and teach them to ride."
(SHE folds the list carefully, puts it back in her purse.)
You see? Lots of choices. *(Pause)* Trouble is, I don't want to do any of them.

TOM: I'll help you find something.

VIRGINIA: Actually I . . . kept something.

TOM: Kept something?

VIRGINIA: I kept this. *(SHE produces the manuscript.)* I promised her I'd burn it. But I didn't. *(Pause)* It was something to hold on to. *(SHE puts it down between them.)* There it is.

TOM: There it is.

VIRGINIA: Do you want it?

TOM: *(This is tough for him.)* No.

VIRGINIA: Are you sure?

TOM: I'm writing my own book now. Strangest thing: the minute I left here I started writing.

VIRGINIA: About Gram?

TOM: No, it's about—I'm not sure what it's about. I have these thoughts—no, I have these feelings, and I came back to work them out. *(Pause)*

VIRGINIA: Would you get a cab then, please?

TOM: O.K. You coming?

VIRGINIA: *(Not moving)* I want to say goodbye.

TOM: All right.

(HE goes Off. SHE looks at her grandmother's chair. Then SHE takes the manuscript and quickly goes into Isabel's room. A moment. Then TOM comes back in. HE stands at the doorway to the hall.)

Virginia?

VIRGINIA'S VOICE: *(From within)* I'll be right there.

TOM: The security guy's getting the cab. He'll ring.

VIRGINIA'S VOICE: Thank you.

TOM: Hey lookit. You're golden now, you know that? You're free and clear. I'll take you around first thing in the morning. Introduce you to an editor at Scribner's. They'll give you a good deal. They used to publish Fitzgerald.

(VIRGINIA comes out from Isabel's room. SHE is empty-handed.)

All set?

VIRGINIA: I hope so. *(Pause)*

TOM: Where's the sacred tome?

VIRGINIA: In there.

TOM: In there?

VIRGINIA: In the fireplace.

(HE looks at her, looks at the doorway where we see a flickering glow. HE starts for the doorway, then reluctantly stops.)

TOM: Oh boy.

VIRGINIA: I know it.

TOM: Did you read it?

VIRGINIA: Cover to cover.

TOM: Was it Fitzgerald?

VIRGINIA: No.

TOM: It was, wasn't it?

VIRGINIA: No.

TOM: I'll bet it was.

VIRGINIA: It was just a play.

TOM: A play?

VIRGINIA: An old melodrama.

TOM: By Walter Babcock McCoy?

VIRGINIA: Exactly. Very old fashioned. Very old hat.

TOM: Was it called *The Golden Age?*

VIRGINIA: Yes! And it ends right here in this room. There's this man and this woman.

TOM: He says he loves her. And wants her to live with him.

VIRGINIA: Ah, but *she* says she had this fabulous grandmother. And she hopes she's inherited some of her . . . spark, I think it was. And then she straightens her shoulders, which she learned to do in posture class at boarding school, and walks right up to the man and shakes hands. *(SHE speaks very softly.)* Goodbye.

TOM: *(Leaning forward to hear)* What? What did you say? *(SHE gestures "nothing!" and walks away.)* Will I see you again?

VIRGINIA: You can bring me your book.

TOM: Not before I make a copy. *(The doorbell rings below.)* There's the cab. Can we share it?

VIRGINIA: Not today. But you could take down my bag. *(SHE starts out.)*

TOM: Can I at least keep the cat?

VIRGINIA: It got out.

TOM: Will it survive?

VIRGINIA: It did before.

TOM: That was a different cat.

VIRGINIA: So am I.

(SHE goes out. TOM goes to pick up her bag as the lights fade on the room.)

CURTAIN

What I Did Last Summer

What I Did Last Summer was first produced as a play-in-progress at the Circle Repertory Company in New York City in November 1981, directed by Porter Van Zandt. It was similarly done at the Seattle Repertory Company in February 1982, directed by Daniel Sullivan.

Its first full production opened at the Cape Playhouse in Dennis, Massachusetts, on August 9, 1982, with the following cast:

CHARLIE ....Mark Arnott
TED ....Tod Waring
GRACE ....Barbara Feldon
ELSIE ....Ellen Parker
BONNY ....Eve Bennett-Gordon
ANNA TRUMBULL ....Eileen Heckart

Melvin Bernhardt was the director, Loren Sherman the designer, Scott Lehrer did the sound, and Denise Romano the costumes. James B. McKenzie was the executive producer, Jack V. Booch, the artistic producer.

It opened in New York at the Circle Repertory Company on February 6, 1983, with the following cast:

CHARLIE..................................Ben Siegler
TED ....Robert Joy
GRACE ....Debra Mooney

ELSIE ....Christine Estabrook
BONNY ....Ann McDonough
ANNA TRUMBULL ....Jacqueline Brookes

John Lee Beatty designed the set, Jennifer Von Mayrhauser the costumes, Craig Miller the lighting, and Chuck London the sound. The production stage manager was Suzanne Fry.

CAST

CHARLIE, fourteen★
TED, sixteen, Charlie's friend★
GRACE, Charlie's mother
ELSIE, nineteen, Charlie's sister★
BONNY, fourteen★
ANNA TRUMBULL

Time: Summer 1945

Place: A summer "colony" on the Canadian shore of Lake Erie, near Buffalo, New York.

Set: Simple and presentational. Wooden and wicker furniture, sun-bleached and sandworn, as indicated in ground-plan; a simple wooden glider might serve as a central element, becoming occasionally the front seat of a car. Plenty of sunlight, blue sky, and occasional green shade.

Props: As indicated. In other words, only when it seems simpler to use them than not. For example, the clay in Act I probably is helpful, but plates and glasses for the supper scene probably are not.

Costumes: To be changed or adjusted only when indicated.

*Casting: The young people in this play may be played by
actors older than these indicated ages. In this way, we
will have more of the sense of actors enacting their roles.
Indeed, throughout this play, we should be aware of
things in the process of being fabricated or made: the
characters by actors; the setting by the manipulation of
simple scenic elements; the play itself by its obviously
traditional and presentational form.

ACT ONE

Before Curtain: Music: an old Bing Crosby recording such as "Swinging on a Star." CHARLIE comes in in khakis, T-shirt, and old sneakers, as a fourteen-year-old.

CHARLIE: *(To audience)* This is a play about me when I was fourteen, back during the war, when we had this house at a place called Rose Hill, on the Canadian shore of Lake Erie, near Buffalo, New York, where I was born . . . That was the summer I planned to sit around the house . . . *(HE sits.)* And study Latin, which I flunked in June . . . and sail my dad's cat-boat in the races every Wednesday and Saturday . . . or practice driving my mother's car in the driveway . . . *(The bench might momentarily become a car. HE mimes driving.)* or play tennis on the Wilsons' clay court . . . *(HE is up by now, miming an elaborate serve.)* Pow! and then after a game, me and my friend Ted Moffatt . . .

(TED runs across the stage, in old clothes.)

TED: Bombs away! *(HE exits D.R., whistling like a bomb.)*

CHARLIE: *(Watching him)* . . . would run down the bank to the beach, jumping over the patches of poison ivy, and then dash over the hot sand, and charge through the water out to the sandbar, where you could dive in, and open your mouth, and drink in half the lake, if you wanted to!

TED: *(Shouting, from Off)* Come on, Charlie!

CHARLIE: *(Starting to take off his sneakers)* Prepare to attack! Look out below!

(GRACE comes On from U.L.)

GRACE: Charlie, you stay right where you are! *(SHE is in her late thirties, attractive, in a simple summer dress.)* Nobody's going near that water until they've picked up their room! It's an absolute pigsty!

CHARLIE: *(Holding his sneakers)* Later, Mom.

GRACE: Right now, Charlie!

TED: *(Offstage)* Zowie! The water's great!

CHARLIE: Mom, Ted's *waiting!*

(HE dashes Off, dropping his sneakers Onstage.)

GRACE: Charlie, I'm warning you . . . Charlie, I am issuing an ultimatum! . . . Charlie!

(But he's gone. ELSIE, Charlie's sister, come On from U.L. SHE is nineteen, wears rolled-up blue jeans and a baggy man's shirt. SHE carries a large copy of War and Peace.)

ELSIE: He wouldn't get away with that if Daddy were here.

GRACE: Well Daddy's not here, as we all well know, and so we'll just have to do the best we can without him . . .

(SHE peers out at the lake.)

Oh now honestly.

ELSIE: What?

GRACE: *(Peering)* Are those boys . . . wearing . . . their bathing suits?

ELSIE: *(Looking out)* Oh God.

GRACE: Are they? or not. I can't tell.

(SHE shades her eyes.)

ELSIE: Wouldn't you know.

GRACE: What?

ELSIE: They're playing "When the Moon Comes over the Mountain."

GRACE: They're playing what?

ELSIE: They're *mooning*, Mother. They think it's an absolute riot. They take everything off, and roll their rear ends around in the waves.

GRACE: Oh don't be silly.

ELSIE: They *do*, Mother. Wait, I'll get the binoculars.

GRACE: That's not necessary, Elsie. *(SHE stares out.)* Why on earth would they want to do a thing like that?

ELSIE: They like to tease the baby-sitters on the beach. Who think it's a perfect scream.

GRACE: Well I don't think it's funny at all.

ELSIE: Neither do I, Mother. And lately do you know what else they've been doing?

GRACE: I'm not interested, thank you.
(SHE starts to pick up the sneakers, stops.)
What?

ELSIE: They fill their athletic supporters full of stones, and then march up and down. All the way to the public beach. With these great bulges in their fronts.

GRACE: Oh honestly.

ELSIE: That's what they do! And it's repulsive, Mother. With women and children around? No one even knows where to look.

GRACE: I'll speak to him.

ELSIE: And here it is just the beginning of summer. Lord knows what he'll be up to by Labor Day.
(SHE settles down to read War and Peace *in the chair.)*

GRACE: We'll just have to think up some projects for him, that's all. We'll have to make a good, long list. Repairing the steps, painting the terrace furniture . . .

ELSIE: Oh God, I can see it now. Paint dripping all over the house . . .

GRACE: Now that's enough, Elsie. I don't see you killing yourself this summer.

ELSIE: Mother!

GRACE: And I think *your* room could stand a little more attention.

ELSIE: Mother, I am busy all the *time*. I'm collecting money for Bundles for Britain, I've started *War and Peace* for summer reading. . . .

GRACE: Well all I know is I don't get much help with the errands.

ELSIE: That's because I can't *drive*, Mother.

GRACE: You *can* drive, Elsie. You've even got your license. You just won't, that's all.

ELSIE: I get nervous, Mother.

GRACE: Well you're not too nervous to pick on your brother every other minute.

ELSIE: But he's so imma*ture*, Mother.

GRACE: Yes well, we all have a little growing to do, now don't we.

ELSIE: Oh, Mother, what a snide thing to say!

GRACE: Yes well . . .

ELSIE: I mean it! I just wish Daddy were here, that's all! That's all I wish!

(SHE storms Off U.L.)

GRACE: *(Looking after her with a sigh)* So do I. Oh boy. So do I.

(SHE picks up Charlie's sneakers as she speaks to the audience.) This is also a play about me, trying to run a house, trying to run two houses, one here, one in town, trying to keep things clean, trying to keep things going, trying to give two children a good healthy summer, away from the city, away from the polio scare, even during the war, with gas coupons, and meat rationing, and you name it, while my husband is away, overseas for eighteen and a half months, somewhere in the Pacific, cooped up on a destroyer escort, when any minute some kamikaze pilot could dive down and blow him to smithereens! . . . *that's* what this play is about, if you ask me! And if it isn't, it should be.

(GRACE *strides Off,* U.L., *carrying Charlie's sneakers, as* CHARLIE *and* TED *come On from* D.R., *snapping towels at each other, as if they were duellists in a movie. They duel all over the stage, peppering their attacks with expressions from comic books.)*

CHARLIE: Shazam!

TED: Pow!

CHARLIE: Ooof!

TED: Whammo!

CHARLIE: Banzai!

TED: Die, Yankee dog!

CHARLIE: Take that . . . and that . . . and that, you Canuck bastard!

*(*TED *suddenly serious, grabs* CHARLIE'S *towel.)*

TED: What did you say?

CHARLIE: I just said—

TED: You called me a Canuck.

CHARLIE: What's wrong with that? You're Canadian, aren't you?

TED: *(Shoving him)* I'm not a Canuck, Charlie!

CHARLIE: *(Shoving him back)* Hey now watch it . . . .

(And suddenly they are wrestling in earnest, puffing and grunting. TED *forces* CHARLIE *to the ground, and tries to pin him.* CHARLIE *writhes and heaves to get out from under.* BONNY *comes On quickly from* U.L. SHE *is pretty and young, wearing an informal summer dress.)*

BONNY: Oh *no!* What *now? (The boys continue to struggle.)* I thought you two were best friends!

TED: Not when he insults a guy.

CHARLIE: *(Still struggling)* He can't take a joke!

BONNY: Let him UP, Ted. He's younger.

TED: First he's got to apologize.

CHARLIE: *(Struggling)* That'll be the day.

BONNY: Oh you're both so juvenile!

TED: *(Trying to pin him)* Come on, Charlie, unconditional surrender!

CHARLIE: Never! You Canuck! *(More intense struggling)*

BONNY: *(Sitting down)* All right. I just wanted to know who could crew for me this afternoon.

(The boys stop fighting and look at her.)

My father's playing golf, so I get to skipper the Snipe.

(TED and CHARLIE jump up.)

TED & CHARLIE: *(Simultaneously)* I'll do it . . . Let me . . .

BONNY: *(To TED)* I thought you had to cut people's grass this summer, Ted. I thought you had a job.

TED: I'll take the afternoon off.

BONNY: You will?

CHARLIE: Yeah, but I know more about sailing. My dad taught me.

BONNY: That's true. Oh help. I'm terrible about making decisions. Hmmm. *(SHE makes the most of the moment.)* Tell you what . . . This time I'll take Ted.

CHARLIE: How *come?*

BONNY: Because he's a working man, Charlie. You're free any time, all summer.

CHARLIE: I'm not. I'm working. I work, too.

TED: Yeah sure. For your mother.

CHARLIE: Well you work for your father.

BONNY: It's not the same thing, Charlie. Ted is personally responsible for a large number of lawns.

CHARLIE: That's because his father is caretaker around here. He gave him the job.

TED: I'd better go check out with him, by the way.

(HE starts Off, D.L.)

CHARLIE: *(Calling after him)* If my dad were home, I'd have a regular job, too. In the city, maybe. We'd drive in together every day. We'd commute!

TED: *(Returning)* Hey, Charlie, why don't you get a job with the Pig Woman? She's got a notice up in Brodie's drugstore.

CHARLIE: Maybe I will.

TED: I hear she doesn't wear any underpants. Might give you a charge.

BONNY: Don't get grubby, please.

CHARLIE: Maybe I will work for her.

TED: Sure. Work for the Pig Woman. Of course, I hear she pays peanuts. Or maybe it's acorns.

(HE goes Off laughing.)

BONNY: Ted's getting very sarcastic this summer.

CHARLIE: Does the Pig Woman really have a notice up in Brodie's?

BONNY: I don't know, Charlie. You shouldn't work for her anyway.

(THEY sit down, side by side, on the glider.)

CHARLIE: Why not?

BONNY: My mother says she's an immoral woman.

CHARLIE: What do you mean, immoral?

BONNY: She used to be somebody's mistress.

CHARLIE: No kidding.

BONNY: She *was!* She was the mistress of some doctor. He kept his wife in town, and brought the Pig Woman out here. And left her that place when he died.

CHARLIE: Ted says she's part Indian.

BONNY: She is! She's got mixed blood. And she's an artist manquée.

CHARLIE: A what?

BONNY: Artist manquée. It means she gives art lessons but nobody takes them.

CHARLIE: Then how can she pay? I mean, if I decide to work for her.

BONNY: I don't know, Charlie. Mother says she's just hanging on, with no visible means of support.

(SHE gets up.)

And now I've got to go sail.

(SHE starts off, R.)

CHARLIE: *(Getting up)* Yeah well thanks a bunch for picking Ted.

BONNY: I tried to be fair, Charlie.

CHARLIE: Yeah fair. Uh huh fair. You didn't even let us draw lots.

BONNY: He has a *job*, Charlie. He needs rest and recreation.

CHARLIE: I think you picked him because he's got his driver's license.

BONNY: Oh stop it.

CHARLIE: I do. I think you want to neck with him. In his car.

BONNY: Oh just grow UP, Charlie. Please!

(SHE goes Off, U.R.)

CHARLIE: *(Shouting after her)* That's what I *think*, Bonny.

(ELSIE comes On from U.L. carrying her War and Peace.*)*

ELSIE: Charlie, Mother's driving to the village, and she needs someone to help with the groceries.

(SHE takes his towel from him.)

CHARLIE: Why don't you go?

ELSIE: Because I've made other PLANS, Charlie.

(SHE spreads the towel out on the platform, D.R., and lies down.)

Now hurry! She's waiting in the car!

(CHARLIE starts shuffling Off.)

God, you're a slob.

CHARLIE: *(Turning, giving her the finger)* Perch and rotate, Elsie. Perch, and systematically rotate, please.

(HE goes Off, U.L.)

ELSIE: Oh Jesus, you're disgusting.

(The lights dim on ELSIE reading, as GRACE comes on from U.R., briskly, carrying a paper bag. SHE stops, looks over her shoulder.)

GRACE: *(To audience)* Now where'd he go? I left him right by the cash register.

(CHARLIE comes On from U.R., carrying another grocery bag.)

CHARLIE: I dropped the eggs.

GRACE: Oh, Charlie.

CHARLIE: It's O.K. They gave me more.

GRACE: Well let's get things into this car before the ice cream melts.

(THEY unload the groceries into the "trunk" of the glider.)

Where'd you go earlier? I thought you wanted to pick out the cookies.

CHARLIE: I just went to Brodie's, Mom.

GRACE: To read the funny books?

CHARLIE: No, not to read the "funny" books, Mom. I don't read "funny" books any more.

GRACE: Then what was that I found under your bed?

CHARLIE: That was Classic *Comics*, Mom. For school. *A Tale of Two Cities.*

GRACE: Well I don't consider it a tale of two anything. I threw it out.

CHARLIE: Oh boy. You would.

(THEY close the "trunk," come around either side to get into the "car." THEY talk over the "top.")

GRACE: Did you at least stop by the post office?

CHARLIE: Of course.

GRACE: Anything?

CHARLIE: I would have told you, Mom.

GRACE: Oh dear.

CHARLIE: It's been five weeks since we heard.

GRACE: Oh well now we mustn't brood. He's on a ship. You wait. Soon there'll be a great stack of letters. For all of us.

(THEY get into the "car." GRACE sits for a moment before starting it.)

I have a bone to pick with you.

CHARLIE: What?

GRACE: When Mr. McAlister came up by the cash register, you were very rude.

CHARLIE: Who? Boris?

GRACE: Mr. McAlister to you, please.

CHARLIE: He looks like Boris. Of Karloff fame.

GRACE: Well for your information, he happens to be one of the most attractive men in Buffalo.

CHARLIE: He's always hanging around you.

GRACE: Don't be silly.

CHARLIE: He is. He's always coming up.

GRACE: He's a very lonely man.

CHARLIE: Yeah, yeah.

GRACE: You just don't know, Charlie. His son was killed in Italy. His wife is in the hospital with a nervous breakdown—

CHARLIE: Well all I know is he's all over you like a tent.

GRACE: Oh, Charlie . . .

CHARLIE: He's a son of a beech . . . (GRACE *wheels on him.*) . . . nut tree.

(GRACE *starts the "car," and mimes driving, very simply. No gear-shifting or foot-pedaling is necessary. Using the "wheel" should be enough. The glider might rock back and forth very simply.*)

By the way, I might get a job this summer.

GRACE: We'll think up plenty of jobs.

CHARLIE: I mean a real job.

GRACE: We'll think up a big project.

CHARLIE: I don't mean working for my mother.

GRACE: What did you have in mind then, Charlie?

CHARLIE: There's a notice on Brodie's bulletin board: "Man wanted. Odd Jobs."

GRACE: All right. Try that. Where?

CHARLIE: Black Point.

GRACE: How will you get there? With gas rationing? I can't chauffeur you all over the lakeshore.

CHARLIE: I'll ride my bike.

GRACE: Now that's good, Charlie. That's very enterprising. Daddy would be proud. *(THEY drive.)* Whom will you be working for, by the way?

CHARLIE: Huh?

GRACE: Don't say "huh," Charlie. Cavemen say "huh."

CHARLIE: I didn't hear your question, Mother dear.

GRACE: I said, whom will you be working for?

CHARLIE: The Pig Woman.

GRACE: Who?

CHARLIE: Anna Trumbull. The Pig Woman. It's her notice up in Brodie's. *(Pause)*

GRACE: I don't think so, Charlie.

CHARLIE: Why not?

GRACE: I don't think that's a good idea. At all.

CHARLIE: Would you mind telling me why the hell not?

GRACE: Don't swear, please, Charlie. *(Pause)* She's a disturbing woman, that's why.

CHARLIE: What d'ya mean, disturbing?

GRACE: She's unsettling, Charlie. She likes to rock the boat. Like some people I know.

CHARLIE: It's a job, Mom!

GRACE: Charlie, you flunked Latin. You have to tutor Latin every Tuesday.

CHARLIE: I'll do that, too!

GRACE: Well, the answer is No, Charlie. N.O. And that's final. *(SHE looks out.)* Oh look. Look at the corn. It's not as high as an elephant's eye, but I'll bet we'll be having corn on the cob before you know it.

CHARLIE: Big deal.

GRACE: Your favorite thing. Mmmm. Yummy.

CHARLIE: Goodie goodie gum-drop, rah-rah.

(SHE glances at him. THEY drive for a moment in silence. Finally.)

Can I drive? Can I at least do that?

GRACE: No you may not.

CHARLIE: Why not?

GRACE: Because it's against the law, Charlie.

CHARLIE: Ted drives.

GRACE: Well he shouldn't.

CHARLIE: Well he does.

GRACE: Well that's because he's Canadian. They do things differently . . . *(SHE looks out.)* There are the Robinsons. Wave to the Robinsons! Hi, hi!
(SHE waves as they go by. CHARLIE gives them the finger out his window.)

CHARLIE: It's just back roads, Mom.

GRACE: I don't care if it's back roads or Delaware Avenue.

CHARLIE: I've been practicing in our driveway.

GRACE: That's not the open highway.

CHARLIE: Please, Mom.

GRACE: I'm sorry.

CHARLIE: You never let me do anything.

GRACE: I don't let you kill yourself, no.

CHARLIE: You wouldn't even let me have a beer at the Potters'.

GRACE: Not at fourteen, no.

CHARLIE: You're a real wet blanket, Mom. All the time.

GRACE: Who took you and your friends to the movies, just the other night?

CHARLIE: Took us. TOOK us. You wouldn't even let us hitchhike.

GRACE: Not at night. No.

CHARLIE: And we had to see *your* movie. We had to see *Mrs. Miniver* again, for Chrissake.

GRACE: I've asked you not to swear, please.

CHARLIE: *(Softly, out the window)* Yeah well go to hell.
(GRACE slams on the "brakes." THEY both rock suddenly forward.)

GRACE: What did you say?

CHARLIE: Never mind.

GRACE: What did you *say?*

CHARLIE: *(Grimly)* I said "Go to hell."

GRACE: Out of the car.

CHARLIE: Oh, Mom . . .

GRACE: Out. Right now. People who swear at their mothers can learn to walk the rest of the way home.

CHARLIE: I was just—

GRACE: OUT, Charlie. Right now. I mean it.

(SHE leans grimly across him, and opens his "door." CHARLIE groans, gets out of the "car," slams the door, walks a little way off. GRACE starts the car forward. CHARLIE fades U. SHE stops the car, and sits for a moment, staring ahead. CHARLIE watches her. SHE relents, calls to him, opens the door.)

Come on.

(CHARLIE approaches the "car" sullenly, and gets back in, closing the "door." GRACE starts the "car" forward. Finally.)

Honestly, Charlie, I'm at the end of my rope, I miss Daddy so much, I'm trying so hard to keep things going, and the last thing I need is you being rude to my friends or swearing at me in the car.

CHARLIE: I didn't—

GRACE: You did, Charlie. And you're not much help around the house, either. You leave your breakfast dishes all over the kitchen, and you use twice as much butter as you're supposed to, and I find damp, sandy towels all over your bedroom floor. And I notice that Hitchcock chair by your bed is broken again.

CHARLIE: I'll fix it, Mom.

GRACE: You can't, Charlie. And you can't fix that sugar bowl you broke either. There are special men who do that, and they're all away in the war . . . Well anyway . . . *(SHE pulls up.)* Here we are. *(SHE turns, looks at him.)* I'm just asking you to be more helpful, Charlie.

CHARLIE: O.K., Mom.

(HE *starts to get out of the "car."*)

GRACE: Wait, Charlie. One more thing . . . Now this is awkward, but your father is not around, so it's up to me to say it . . . If ever you have . . . an accident at night, Charlie . . . if ever you have what is known as a nocturnal emission (CHARLIE *puts a hand in front of his face.*), *don't* throw the bedsheets over it and pretend that nothing's happened. Change the *sheets*, Charlie. Or tell me. And I'll change them. (*Long pause. HE sits, ultimately humiliated.*) Did you hear me, sweetheart?

CHARLIE: Oh . . . My . . . God!

GRACE: I'm sorry, darling, but I thought I should bring it up.

CHARLIE: (*Jumping out of the "car"*) That does it!

GRACE: Oh now . . .

CHARLIE: That really DOES it, Mom!

(HE *starts Off.*)

GRACE: Where are you going?

CHARLIE: To get a job with the Pig Woman!

GRACE: Oh no you're not!

CHARLIE: Oh yes I am!

(HE *runs Off.*)

GRACE: (*Calling after him*) You come back here and unload this car!

CHARLIE: (*From Offstage*) Let Elsie do it!

GRACE: (*Calling*) Charlie!

(ELSIE, *sitting up from her sunbathing* D.R., *as the lights come on her again*)

ELSIE: Let Elsie do what?

GRACE: (*Opening the "trunk"*) Help with the groceries, please.

ELSIE: Why can't Charlie?

GRACE: (*Picking up a grocery bag*) Don't argue, Elsie. Just do it, please. Just do it right now.

(SHE starts off. ELSIE begins to poke around in the remaining bag.)

ELSIE: Did you get melon, Mother? I see cookies for Charlie, but I don't see melon for me. How am I supposed to lose weight if you don't even get any melon? *(SHE looks up, sees that GRACE has gone, U.L. turns to audience.)* Oh boy. I'll tell you one thing this play is *not* about. It's not about *me*. It's not about how it feels to grow up during a war when all the boys your age are away. And you can't even go visit your friends from college because "this trip isn't really necessary." And it's not about how someone can miss her father terribly, and how she dreams about him at night, and how he taught her to drive a car, and gave her the confidence to do it, and now he's not around, she's scared even to try. So what does she do with her summer? She sits around, and gripes, and reads, and smokes, and argues, and EATS! And turns herself into a big, fat, slobby PIG!

(SHE starts Off.)

That's what this play is not about, if anyone wants to know.

(SHE goes Off, U.L. Lights might change to give a greener and leafier effect.)

CHARLIE: *(From Off L.)* Hello? *(No answer. HE calls louder.)* Anybody here? *(CHARLIE comes on, from L.)* Hello!

(ANNA TRUMBULL, the Pig Woman, comes on from U.R., as if from around the corner of her cottage. SHE wears an old, paint-spattered smock, sneakers with holes cut in them for her corns, ankle socks falling around them, and a strange bandana on her head. Her hair is cut in bangs, and straight all around. Her skin is swarthy and sunburned. There is no way of telling her age.)

ANNA: Scram.

CHARLIE: I just want to—

ANNA: Are you one of those boys who threw crabapples at me from the old orchard?

CHARLIE: No!

ANNA: You sure?

CHARLIE: I never hit you.

ANNA: Get off my land.

CHARLIE: I just want to ask you something.

ANNA: The answer is no.

CHARLIE: Wait till I ask!

ANNA: No, I do not have any tin cans for the war effort.

CHARLIE: I'm not collecting tin cans.

ANNA: Then what?

CHARLIE: I read your notice . . . At Brodie's . . . "Man wanted. Odd jobs."

ANNA: Oh that. I put that up in March.

CHARLIE: It's still there.

ANNA: Tell them to take it down.

CHARLIE: You found a man?

ANNA: I did not. There are no men to be found. And where do you think they are? Shooting, maiming, killing each other in all four corners of the globe.

CHARLIE: My father's in the Pacific.

ANNA: I'm sure he is.

CHARLIE: So can I work for you?

ANNA: You?

CHARLIE: Me.

ANNA: What can you do?

CHARLIE: Me?

ANNA: You.

CHARLIE: I can cut your grass.

ANNA: What grass? Do you see any grass around here?

CHARLIE: No.

ANNA: Grass. The very idea galls me. The very notion. Think about grass. Have you ever thought about it?

CHARLIE: No.

ANNA: Then do. Think. Question your assumptions. Think of what grass requires. Think of the topsoil, think of the fertilizer, think of the precious water. Have you ever thought about that?

CHARLIE: No.

ANNA: Have you ever thought of the poor human souls who spend their lives planting it and rolling it and keeping it trim?

CHARLIE: My friend Ted cuts grass.

ANNA: There you are. Think of that.

CHARLIE: I will.

ANNA: And think of the history of grass. Explore its origins. Do you know where it came from?

CHARLIE: No.

ANNA: Grass came directly from the English aristocracy. They thought it up, in order to play their silly games. They bred it and fed it and put signs on it saying keep off it. Got the picture? Wherever there's grass, there's class. Will you remember that? Remember I told you?

CHARLIE: Yes.

ANNA: Good. Then the day's not lost.

(SHE *starts Off* U.R.)

CHARLIE: I could do something else, though.

ANNA: *(Wheeling on him)* Can you put in plumbing? Can you dig a ditch all the way out to the new sewer line? Can you put in pipes? Can you pay for them?

CHARLIE: No.

ANNA: Can you fix a pump?

CHARLIE: I fixed the fuel pump on our Ford station wagon.

ANNA: I don't care about cars.

CHARLIE: What about that old car I saw in your barn?

ANNA: It doesn't work any more.

CHARLIE: I could try and fix it.

ANNA: I don't want a car. I've learned to get along without one.

(SHE *starts Off* R. *again.)*

CHARLIE: Then I could do something *else.* You could teach me.

(SHE *stops, turns.*)

ANNA: How old are you?

CHARLIE: Sixteen. *(Pause)* A year from next November.

ANNA: Which means what?

CHARLIE: Fourteen.

ANNA: A babe. A mere babe. Where are you from?

CHARLIE: Up the beach. Rose Hill.

ANNA: A lost boy. From the Fort. Who's wandered into Indian territory . . . Did you know I had Indian blood?

CHARLIE: Yes.

ANNA: My great-grandmother was a Tuscarora Indian princess.

CHARLIE: Oh.

ANNA: My father was vice-president of the Erie County Street Railway Corporation. I'll bet you didn't know that.

CHARLIE: No.

ANNA: Did you know that my cottage was once a pigsty?

CHARLIE: No.

ANNA: Oh yes. That's why they call me the Pig Woman. Do you think it suits me?

CHARLIE: Um . . .

ANNA: Don't answer that. I like the name. It sets me off. It makes me different. Does that frighten you?

CHARLIE: No. *(Pause)*

ANNA: When could you work?

CHARLIE: Any time. *(Pause)* Except Wednesday and Saturday afternoons.

ANNA: Why not then?

CHARLIE: That's when they have the sailing races.

ANNA: Goodbye.

CHARLIE: I have to. I signed up.

ANNA: I refuse to accommodate myself to the leisure class.

CHARLIE: I'll work every morning for you.

ANNA: Every morning?

CHARLIE: Except Tuesdays.

ANNA: 'Scram. Vamoose.

CHARLIE: I have to tutor on Tuesdays.

ANNA: Bye-bye.

CHARLIE: I flunked Latin! I have to tutor!

ANNA: Back to Rose Hill! Back to the stockade, white man!
   (SHE *goes Off* R.)

CHARLIE: *(Calling after her)* O.K. I'll work it OUT. I'll quit
   the sailing, if I can have the job.
   (Pause; SHE *comes back on.)*

ANNA: I can see you're willing to make a momentous sacri-
   fice . . . All right. I'll hire you.

CHARLIE: Thanks.

ANNA: I'll give you twenty-five cents an hour.

CHARLIE: Huh?

ANNA: Twenty-five.

CHARLIE: That's all?

ANNA: That's enough for a beginner.

CHARLIE: My friend Ted gets fifty.

ANNA: For what?

CHARLIE: Cutting grass.

ANNA: You see what grass does to the economy?

CHARLIE: I got twenty-five cents two *years* ago just for
   walking the Watsons' dog.

ANNA: I know that dog. That dog isn't worth a dime.

CHARLIE: Well I just can't work for twenty-five cents an
   hour. I just can't.

ANNA: Well I just can't afford to pay you anything more.
   Sorry.

CHARLIE: Which means I got to go back to Rose Hill and tell
   everybody and his uncle I couldn't get a job, and take a
   lot of crap from my mother and my sister, and listen to
   Ted sling the bull all summer, and feel like a baby in front
   of Bonny! Darn it! Darn it all! Damn it! Goddammit to hell!
   (HE turns and starts Off L.)

ANNA: Stop! *(HE does.)* Come here! *(HE does.)* Let me see your hands.

CHARLIE: *(Stopping)* My hands?

ANNA: Let me see them.

(CHARLIE wipes his hands on his pants, then holds them up. ANNA crosses, takes them, looks them over.)

You have very expressive hands.

CHARLIE: I do?

ANNA: You also have strong feelings.

CHARLIE: I sure do.

ANNA: *(Dropping his hands)* Because of your hands, and your feelings, I have decided to give you more than twenty-five cents an hour.

CHARLIE: Hey, thanks.

ANNA: I've decided to give you art lessons.

CHARLIE: Art lessons?

ANNA: I will root out your talent, wherever it lies. I will teach you to express your feelings with your hands.

CHARLIE: Every day?

ANNA: Every afternoon. And what you will get from me will be worth far more than money. Now make up your mind. Work here on these terms, or run back to Rose Hill and tell them you turned down a chance to build your body and stretch your soul with Anna Trumbull, the Pig Woman.

CHARLIE: *(Finally)* I'll do it. *(SHE sits, indicates that HE is to sit beside her.)*

ANNA: Good. You will arrive every morning at eight o'clock. I'll probably be asleep. Walk right in and give me a good shake. I sleep soundly because I have such delicious dreams. My lover, old Doctor Holloway, used to wake me with a kiss. No need for you to do that. Just hand me a cup of strong, hot coffee, and then we will proceed to labor in the vineyards together.

CHARLIE: O.K.

ANNA: We will work primarily out of doors, in the soil, in the sun. At noon, we will swim off the rocks in my cove. Bring your bathing suit or not, as you see fit. I don't wear one myself. I find them inhibiting. Do you?

CHARLIE: Um . . .

ANNA: Never mind. It's not important. After our swim we will have lunch. I will provide it. It will consist of home-made bread, unprocessed cheese, and fruit in season. And one glass of good red wine. Do you have any trouble with wine?

CHARLIE: No.

ANNA: I do. Because of my Indian blood, I have a weakness for alcohol. I hope you'll keep an eye on me in that department.

CHARLIE: O.K.

ANNA: Good. And while we eat, we will sit in the shade and talk. I will tell you about town. I grew up there, and think of it with all the passion of an exile. Would you like to hear me rail against your homeland?

CHARLIE: Sure.

ANNA: Then you've come to the right place . . . But in the afternoon, we will get serious. We will create things together. We will seek patterns, we will make shapes, we will fabricate visions of a better world. Is that all clear?

CHARLIE: Yes, Miss Trumbull.

ANNA: Call me Anna, since we are to be colleagues in life and art.

(THEY get up.)

CHARLIE: O.K., Anna.

ANNA: And what do I call you?

CHARLIE: Charlie. Charlie Higgins.

ANNA: Higgins. I knew the Higgins family. Stuffy bunch, all the way down the line. Loved money, hated horses, never knew what to do about women.

CHARLIE: That's me.

ANNA: One of them married a girl named Grace Anderson.

CHARLIE: That's my mom.

ANNA: No!

CHARLIE: Sure. She's my mother.

ANNA: *(Bursting into laughter)* Oh boy. Ohboyohboyohboy-ohboy. That's a pip. That's a lulu. The chickens come home to roost. Does she know you're here?

CHARLIE: Sort of.

ANNA: "Sort of." I'll bet "sort of." *(SHE laughs again.)* Well we'll see you tomorrow, Charlie. *If* we see you tomorrow.

(SHE goes Off R., laughing, shaking her head. CHARLIE stands looking after her, then goes Off slowly in the opposite direction, as BONNY comes out from U.R., carrying a towel, calling Offstage as SHE enters.)

BONNY: All right! It's an hour after lunch! Everybody can go in the water! *(BONNY spreads the towel, as if she were on a beach. SHE speaks quietly to the audience.)* Sometimes I think this play is secretly about me. That's what I secretly think. Because, for me, this is a crucial summer. All sorts of important things are beginning to happen. My father's letting me skipper the boat occasionally. And my mother says I can smoke, as long as it's in front of her. And I've got a paid baby-sitting job three times a week. *(SHE calls out.)* It's not cold, Susie. Just go in slowly. Bit by bit. And it'll feel fine. *(To audience)* And tonight, one of the most crucial things of all might happen. Tonight we might be riding this roller coaster. It's called The Cyclone, and on a calm night you can hear it roar, even though the amusement park is over five miles away! Oh it's the scariest thing! It's built right out over the lake, all rickety and shaky, and they say when you climb to the top, you can see all the way to town. And when you start down, it's so basically terrifying that *women* have thrown their *babies* over the *side!* It costs five tickets per person per ride, and there's a big sign right at the gate saying you have to be at least sixteen before you can ride it. But Ted knows the Canadian boys who take tickets, and right now he's seeing if they can sneak us on. *(Calls out)* Nobody goes out beyond the sandbar, please! Stay in the shallow water where I can see you! *(TED comes on eagerly, from* U.L.*)*

TED: Everything's copasetic.

BONNY: They'll let us on.

TED: No problem.

BONNY: Oh I'm shaking like a leaf. Did you tell Charlie?

TED: How could I tell Charlie? He's over at the Pig Woman's again.

BONNY: We'll have to wait and see if he can come too.

TED: Why Charlie?

BONNY: Because last summer we all promised to ride it together.

TED: They won't let him on. He's too young.

BONNY: He's my age.

TED: That's different. I told them you were my girl.

BONNY: Your *girl*?

TED: So they'd let you through.

BONNY: You mean you didn't mention Charlie?

TED: I said I was bringing my girl.

BONNY: Oh. *(SHE calls out.)* Stay together, everybody! Everybody stay close together! *(Pause)*

TED: So what do you say?

BONNY: How would we get there?

TED: How do you think? By car.

BONNY: With you driving? Or your father?

TED: I got my license, remember?

BONNY: I can't, then.

TED: How come?

BONNY: My mother doesn't want me to go out alone at night in cars with older boys. She was even mad I took you sailing with me.

TED: That wasn't a car. And it wasn't at night.

BONNY: Well I don't know. She thinks you're too old for me.

TED: She didn't think that last summer.

BONNY: Well maybe you weren't last summer. *(Calling out)* Yes I saw, Susie! I saw you do that somersault! That was very good, Susie.

TED: Don't tell her then.

BONNY: Don't *tell* her?

TED: Just meet me out by the main road.

BONNY: Without Charlie?

TED: Look, Charlie's going his way, why can't we go ours? Come on. I'll fix it so we ride in the front row. And I'll take you to the frozen custard place afterwards. And introduce you to my whole gang from high school.

BONNY: Gosh . . .

TED: *(Touching her arm)* Sure. It'll be like a date. A real date.

BONNY: You're distracting me, Ted. I'm supposed to be watching these . . . (SHE *looks out at the lake*) . . . kids. (SHE *jumps to her feet.*)
Uh-oh.

TED: What?

BONNY: How many heads to you see out there?

TED: *(Counting quickly)* One . . . two . . . three . . . four . . .

BONNY: There's supposed to be five!

TED: *(Pointing)* And five, over there!

BONNY: Thank God! *(Calling out angrily)* Susie, when you decide to swim underwater, would you *tell* people, please?

TED: Close call, huh?

BONNY: That wouldn't have happened if I had used the buddy system.

TED: I hate the buddy system.

BONNY: Well at least it's safe. *(Clapping her hands.)* Everyone out of the water, please. I'm instigating a new rule! (SHE *starts Off* U.R.)

TED: What about our date?

BONNY: Tell you what: I'll ask my father.

TED: He'll say no.

BONNY: He might not. He lets me do more than my mother.
(SHE goes Off U.R.*)*
New rule, everybody! New rule! We're going to have the
buddy system!
(SHE goes Off.)

TED: *(Calling after her)* Your father will say no! *(To audience)*
Sure he'll say no. Lookit, someday somebody ought to
write a play about a Canadian kid who hangs around
Americans while his dad takes care of their summer homes.
Here's the story: First, he's friends with those kids, trad-
ing comics with them, playing tennis, horsing around on
the raft. Everything's hunky-dory. Then he starts growing hair on his nuts, and what do you know? The plot
thickens. Suddenly when he shows up at the tennis courts,
he gets the fish-eye from Mrs. Putnam for even sitting
down and watching, for Christ sake. And soon he feels
creepy even going down to the beach, like now it's out of
bounds, or something. And then suppose he wants to
take out an American girl. My God, suddenly it's like he
wants to French kiss her, and bang her, and carry her off
to Saskatchewan, all on the first date! I dunno. All I know
is somebody ought to write about it some time.
(ELSIE comes on from L. *and begins to organize the chairs*
C., *and stools* L. *and* R., *for supper. GRACE comes on from* R.,
and helps. No actual table is necessary.)

ELSIE: Where've you been?

GRACE: Oh, just having a quick drink with poor Mr.
McAlister.

ELSIE: Did you ask him what to do about Charlie?

GRACE: I did not. Charlie is our problem, and we can deal
with it by ourselves.

ELSIE: Where is he now, by the way?

GRACE: Out by the hose. Washing his hands. Which were covered with purple paint.

ELSIE: Purple?

GRACE: Don't ask *me* what she has him doing.

ELSIE: I hope you let him have it, Mother. Tonight I hope you read him the riot act. He's been late for dinner ever since he started that stupid job.

GRACE: Sssshhh.

ELSIE: And he's missed two turns to set the table.

GRACE: He'll make it up.

ELSIE: And he ruins the meal, Mother. With all those obnoxious ideas she gives him.

GRACE: Sshh. We have ideas, too. We'll just have to counteract them.

(THEY *sit down,* GRACE *in the chair,* C., ELSIE *on the stool,* R.)

ELSIE: Well I hope tonight you make him do the dishes, at least. Including the pots and pans. Otherwise it isn't fair.

GRACE: Ssshh. (SHE *hears him coming.*) We're just going to have to hold the line, Elsie. As the Marines did on Iwo Jima. Now are we allies in this, or not?

ELSIE: We're allies, Mother.

GRACE: Thank you, dear.

(THEY *shake hands.* CHARLIE *enters from up* R.)
Good evening, Charlie.

CHARLIE: (*Very jauntily*) Hi.

GRACE: Sit down, dear.

CHARLIE: O.K.

(HE *sits on stool,* L.)

GRACE: Pour Charlie some milk, please, Elsie.

(ELSIE *"pours milk" with grim reluctance.*)

CHARLIE: Thanks.

GRACE: (*Serving "food"*) Now, Charlie, am I giving you too much cauliflower? Speak now, or forever hold your peace.

(SHE hands him a "plate"; little patomiming of eating is necessary.)

CHARLIE: What's this other stuff?

GRACE: Chicken croquettes, dear. *(CHARLIE makes a loud barfing sound.)* Now that's enough, please.

CHARLIE: You know what they look like, don't you?

GRACE: We're not interested, Charlie.

ELSIE: We're not interested.

CHARLIE: Dog turds left on the beach.

ELSIE: Make him leave the table, Mother.

GRACE: I'll handle this, Elsie. *(Smiling, to CHARLIE)* Somebody's feeling his oats a little these days. Am I right? Somebody is full of beans these days.

CHARLIE: Maybe.

GRACE: Otherwise you would not have made such an unattractive remark about the food. Which we are lucky to have. Which millions of refugees throughout Europe would give their eye-*teeth* for.

CHARLIE: Send it to 'em.

ELSIE: Brat.

CHARLIE: *(To ELSIE)* Wrap it up, and put it in a Bundle for Britain.

ELSIE: Will you shut *up*?

GRACE: Now stop it, both of you. *(Pause)* I take it you enjoy your new job, Charlie.

CHARLIE: Uh huh.

GRACE: You must, because it seems to occupy so much of your time.

CHARLIE: Uh huh.

GRACE: For example, I hear you missed your Latin lesson last Tuesday.

CHARLIE: Oh yeah.

GRACE: Missed it completely. Without even telephoning Mrs. Blackburn to cancel it.

CHARLIE: Sorry.

GRACE: Even after you promised Daddy you'd study it all summer long.

CHARLIE: I said I was sorry.

GRACE: Even though you might have to stay behind a grade if you don't pass it in the fall.

CHARLIE: I'm studying it on my own.

ELSIE: You haven't cracked a book.

CHARLIE: Well you know why, don't you?

ELSIE: No, why?

CHARLIE: Latin is the language of the leisure class.

GRACE: What?

CHARLIE: It's true. We all study Latin just because the poor people don't have time to.

ELSIE: Oh my God.

GRACE: That is a silly argument, Charlie, and I think I know where it came from.

CHARLIE: Well it's true, anyway.

GRACE: It is not true. Latin is . . . *(CHARLIE and ELSIE look at her expectantly.)* Latin is the basic building block of western civilization. And I don't think we need to discuss it any further.

ELSIE: Thank God.

GRACE: What is she paying you, by the way?

CHARLIE: I prefer not to say.

GRACE: I'll pay you more.

CHARLIE: To do what?

GRACE: Paint the garage.

CHARLIE: No thanks.

GRACE: I'll pay you twice what she pays you.

CHARLIE: No thanks, Mom.

GRACE: I'll just have to get someone else, then.

CHARLIE: O.K.

GRACE: I'll just have to get your friend Ted Moffatt to come over and paint our garage. For a dollar an hour.

ELSIE: *I'll* do it for that. I'll paint it.

GRACE: Stay *out* of this, Elsie. Please. *(Pause)* What do you think of her, Charlie?

CHARLIE: Who? Elsie? She's a drip.

GRACE: I'm talking about Miss Trumbull, Charlie.

CHARLIE: Oh, you mean Anna.

GRACE: Yes. All right. Anna. What do you think?

CHARLIE: I like her.

GRACE: You do?

CHARLIE: We get along fine.

GRACE: Does she know who you are, Charlie?

CHARLIE: Who I *am?*

GRACE: Your name? Does she know the name?

CHARLIE: Oh sure.

GRACE: Did it ring a bell?

CHARLIE: What?

GRACE: When you told her your name, what did she say?

CHARLIE: She said she knew you.

ELSIE: Who knew who?

CHARLIE: Anna knew Mom.

ELSIE: What?

GRACE: Oh heavens. Years ago. For a short time. I took an art class from her.

ELSIE: You never told me that.

CHARLIE: I didn't know you were an artist, Mom.

GRACE: I'm not. Oh I thought I was. I did a few little things with watercolors. Flowers and things. But that's not the point, anyway. The point is, Charlie, that when Daddy went to war, you promised to help.

CHARLIE: I will, Mom.

GRACE: Well I don't see you doing it. I don't see you lifting a finger around here since you started that job.

CHARLIE: I'll do it, Mom. I swear.

(HE gets up, starts to take his "plate" Off L.*)*

GRACE: You haven't even cut the grass.

CHARLIE: *(Wheeling on her)* I don't believe in grass.

ELSIE: Oh, my God!

CHARLIE: Have you ever questioned your assumptions about grass?

ELSIE: Have you ever questioned your assumptions about setting the table?

GRACE: Now stop it!

CHARLIE: We should plow that lawn up! We should use it for growing vegetables! We should fertilize it with our own wastes!

ELSIE: See, Mother, how repulsive he is!

GRACE: Charlie, that's enough! Now all I know is you can't do all the things you have to do for me, and still work for Anna Trumbull!

CHARLIE: You mean, quit?

GRACE: That's what I mean.

CHARLIE: But I like her.

GRACE: Charlie, I am asking you, as a special favor, if not for me, then for your father, to give up that job. Will you, Charlie? For your father? Who's away at war?

(CHARLIE *looks at her, then goes Off* L., *carrying his "plate." GRACE asks ELSIE.*) What does that mean?

ELSIE: Don't ask me. I only live here.

GRACE: Oh dear.

ELSIE: Some Iwo Jima, Mother.

GRACE: The battle's not over yet, Elsie.

(CHARLIE *comes back in and sits down.*)

CHARLIE: What's for dessert?

GRACE: I'll tell you when I hear your answer, Charlie.

CHARLIE: The answer is no.

GRACE: I am asking you, please.

CHARLIE: No!

GRACE: All right, Charlie, then from here on in, unless you want real trouble, I expect your room to be immaculate, and the chores done thoroughly, and a new chapter of

Latin learned every single day! And if Miss Trumbull complains about your time, you tell her that your first responsibility is to your family.

CHARLIE: She says my first responsibility is to myself!

GRACE: Well she's wrong.

CHARLIE: She says the family is a dying social unit!

GRACE: She is just plain wrong!

CHARLIE: She says family pressure causes half the misery in the world, and you ought to know it more than anyone!

GRACE: Well you tell her . . . You tell her from me . . . *(Pause)* Oh honestly—
(SHE throws down her "napkin," turns, and strides off, U.L. Pause.)

ELSIE: Now you've done it. I hope she sits down and writes Daddy a long letter. All about you!

CHARLIE: Oh gee.

ELSIE: She made the dessert especially for you, too. Cookie pudding. With whipped cream.

CHARLIE: Oh God, what'll I do?

ELSIE: First you better do those dishes, Charlie.

CHARLIE: O.K.

ELSIE: Including the pots and pans.

CHARLIE: O.K., O.K.

ELSIE: And then you better go up and knock on her door and apologize. The way Daddy used to do.

CHARLIE: O.K.

ELSIE: And you better have your Latin book right in your hand.

CHARLIE: Good idea.

ELSIE: And you better say you're quitting the Pig Woman!

CHARLIE: Never!

ELSIE: Then God help us all!
(SHE goes Off, as the lights change to ANNA's mottled world. SHE comes on from U.R., carrying an old galvanized tub.)

ANNA: *(Calling to Charlie)* Look what I got from the lake.

CHARLIE: *(Leaving the table, moving the chair)* I fixed your chair, Anna!

ANNA: Good! All the more reason to look here.

(SHE places the tub on something, and regards it reverently.) What do you think this is?

CHARLIE: *(Looking in)* Mud.

ANNA: Mud? It's not mud at all. Clay! Good, thick, red Lake Erie clay! Which I dredged up from under a rock, like an Indian maiden, diving for pearls.

(SHE sits, D.R.)

CHARLIE: Oh.

ANNA: Is that all you can say? Just "Oh."

CHARLIE: *(Lying down, stretching)* I'm kind of tired today, Anna. I had to do extra chores for my mother.

ANNA: That's exactly why I brought you this. Touch it. Feel it.

(CHARLIE sits up, begins to dip his fingers into the tub, very gingerly at first.)

Go on. Dig in. Get your hands dirty. Squeeze it. Knead it. Make it ooze.

(HE tries.)

How does it feel?

CHARLIE: Good.

ANNA: Of course it does. It's the muck of life. It's the primal sludge. Work it around for a while. Perhaps we'll discover you're a sculptor.

CHARLIE: You don't think I'm a painter?

ANNA: I've decided you're not.

CHARLIE: I told you I wasn't.

ANNA: Well you tried. I appreciate that. But last night, I reviewed your entire *oeuvre* since you arrived, and I've decided I don't like it. There was only one drawing which had energy and vitality. And that had to do with airplanes.

CHARLIE: That was a Grumman Wildcat attacking a Japanese Zero over the Coral Sea.

ANNA: Whatever. I put it aside, with the rest. I did not come into this world to encourage young people to portray death and destruction. Try sculpture instead.

CHARLIE: How do you know I'm a sculptor?

ANNA: I know you're something. The problem is simply bringing it out.

CHARLIE: Maybe I'm a mechanic. I wish you'd let me fix your car.

ANNA: Cars come and go. Planes rise and fall. I want you to do something more permanent . . . Now get at this clay.

CHARLIE: I can't decide what to make.

ANNA: Make a man. Make yourself.

CHARLIE: I don't feel much like a man.

ANNA: Good God, what are you saying?

CHARLIE: I dunno. I flunked Latin, I don't have my driver's license, Bonny treats me like her little brother. Sometimes I think I'll never be a man.

ANNA: Good heavens. Being a man or a woman isn't any of those things. It's simply realizing your potential.

CHARLIE: You think I've got some?

ANNA: I think everyone does. Even Hitler. But most people never find the right way to work it out. And then there's trouble.

CHARLIE: Have you found a way of working out yours?

ANNA: Of course.

CHARLIE: Then how come I never see you making anything?

ANNA: I'm making something right now.

CHARLIE: Huh?

ANNA: Work that clay, please.

(CHARLIE *works the clay;* ANNA *basks in the sun.*)

CHARLIE: Anna?

ANNA: Mmm?

CHARLIE: If I hadn't shown up, would you have looked for another kid?

ANNA: They have to come to me.

CHARLIE: Do lots of people come to you?

ANNA: No. Not many. Some. Your mother did. But she didn't stay.

CHARLIE: Why not?

ANNA: I'm too dangerous.

CHARLIE: Yeah, dangerous. That's a good one, dangerous.

ANNA: I am, Charlie. Because I'm a great teacher. And all great teachers are dangerous. Such as Socrates. Or Christ. Or me.

CHARLIE: Don't be conceited, Anna.

ANNA: Yes well, ask your mother how dangerous I am.

CHARLIE: Oh hell, she thinks even comic books are dangerous.

ANNA: Yes well, keep working.

CHARLIE: *(As he works)* Maybe next summer, some other kid will come around with more potential.

ANNA: I won't be here next summer.

CHARLIE: Sure you will.

ANNA: Oh no. I've put my ear to the ground, and I hear the cavalry coming.

CHARLIE: What cavalry?

ANNA: Never mind, but they'll be here, Charlie. So you're my last hope. Now let's see what you've done.

CHARLIE: Not much, actually.

ANNA: It lacks commitment . . . We'll have to liberate your spirit. We'll tune up on my tomatoes.

CHARLIE: Your toma*htoes*? Again?

ANNA: My toma*ytoes*, please. They're a vulgar fruit. Use the vulgar pronunciation.

CHARLIE: We've already talked about your tomaytoes.

ANNA: Then let's see how much you remember.

CHARLIE: Your seeds go way, way back.

ANNA: Yes.

CHARLIE: They came from your great-grandmother who was an Indian princess . . .

ANNA: Yes . . .

CHARLIE: And she got them from her lover, who was a French trapper . . .

ANNA: Yes. Who rowed them across the Niagara gorge . . .

CHARLIE: And so they've come down to you . . .

ANNA: Generation by generation . . .

CHARLIE: *(With more enthusiasm)* And they'll last beyond you, too . . .

ANNA: Exactly. Because they're perennials. See? All the little buds are beginning. Soon we'll have flowers, and then fruit. Most people do what at this point?

CHARLIE: They pinch them and stake them and prune them.

ANNA: But not me . . .

CHARLIE: You let them grow any way they want . . .

ANNA: And all, all will bear fruit, as long as they get plenty of water, plenty of sun and plenty of . . .

BOTH: Good, honest shit!

ANNA: *(SHE bends down.)* Here. I'll pinch off a shoot. *(SHE brings it to him.)* Smell that. Inhale it deep into your lungs . . . Now close your eyes, and keep working . . . *(HE does.)* That's the smell of old France, and Canada, and the Niagara Frontier . . . At the end of the summer, I plan to give you some of my seeds. Some day, some other summer, you will have the pleasure of picking a ripe tomato from one of my plants. First, you will simply weigh it in the palm of your hand. Then you will admire its shape and color. Suddenly you will close your eyes and mash it into your mouth. You'll let the juice spill out, and the meat roll around on your tongue, and then you'll swallow— meat, juice, seeds, and all. And then you'll open your eyes, open them wide, and give out a great, loud war-whoop of praise to life, and the noble tomato, and to me, Anna Trumbull, the Pig Woman, who introduced you to it.

(SHE crosses to him)
And now let's see what you've done.
(SHE takes up his work, looks at it.) Hmmm.

CHARLIE: It keeps collapsing.

ANNA: Mmmm.

CHARLIE: Maybe I'm not a sculptor either.

ANNA: Of course you are. I'll tell you what you've made. What you've made is a spectacular ashtray, that's what you've made. If I smoked, I'd use it continuously. In fact, it's so good I'm thinking of taking up smoking.

CHARLIE: You're just trying to make me feel better.

ANNA: Well what's wrong with that? Go wash off in the lake while I fix lunch, and then we'll try again.
(THEY start Off R.)

CHARLIE: After lunch, can't I work on your car? Maybe *that's* my potential.

ANNA: Nonsense. After lunch we'll try working with wood.

CHARLIE: Oh Anna . . .

ANNA: And if wood doesn't work, we'll try something else. We'll keep plugging, you and I, on into the night.

CHARLIE: I'm going out with my friends tonight.

ANNA: *(As they exit, R.)* Well then we'll seize the day. And if you work hard, I will tell you the story of my cucumbers. There is an amusing anecdote connecting them to the sexual member of my lover, old Doctor Holloway. I think you're man enough to hear it.
(THEY exit, R., CHARLIE carrying the tub. TED comes on from U.L. singing "Pistol Packin' Mama." HE gets into his "car," adjusts the "mirror," combs his hair, and then waits impatiently. BONNY backs On nervously from U.L.)

TED: *(Rolling down the "window", leaning out)* Come on.

BONNY: He's not here yet.

TED: Who? Don't tell me you asked Charlie!

BONNY: He said he'd meet me in the driveway right after supper.

TED: You and your buddy system . . . You'd think a guy could ask a girl for a date without her bringing along another guy.

BONNY: Charlie's not just another guy.

TED: Do you think you could at least wait for him in the car? Or would your dad think you were necking with a Canuck?

BONNY: I can wait in the car, Ted.

(TED *gets out, crosses around the front and opens the door for her. SHE gets in uneasily. SHE sneaks a peek in the "mirror" while he crosses back.*)

TED: (*Getting into the "car"*) Did you tell your folks you were going to the Cyclone?

BONNY: I decided not to. I told them we were all going to see *Dumbo*.

TED: "All." I love that "all."

BONNY: They're at least letting me drive in your car, Ted. That's something, at least.

TED: Yeah well, look. Here comes your buddy.

(CHARLIE *comes on from* U.L.)

CHARLIE: Sorry.

TED: Where were you?

CHARLIE: I fell asleep.

TED: At eight in the evening?

CHARLIE: I was tired. O.K.? I've been working for two women.

(CHARLIE *starts to get in next to* BONNY. TED *reaches behind* BONNY, *to pull forward the "seat."*)

TED: Get in back, O.K.?

CHARLIE: How come I can't sit in front?

TED: It's a floor gearshift. Get in back.

BONNY: He's just gotten his license, Charlie.

TED: I just want him in back.

BONNY: Be reasonable, Charlie.

(CHARLIE *reluctantly gets into the back, shoving* BONNY *forward by the "seat."* BONNY *closes the "door."*)

TED: And we are off. To the Cyclone! (HE *starts up the "car."*)

CHARLIE: *(Leaning forward, between them)* Don't you think you better put on you lights first, Ted?

TED: *(Quickly putting the "lights" on)* I was planning to do that.

CHARLIE: *(Sitting back)* Oh yeah. Sure. Right. You bet. *(THEY drive.)*

TED: So, Charlie. How's the Pig Woman?

CHARLIE: Fine.

TED: Is it true she doesn't wear any underpants?

BONNY: Oh honestly . . .

CHARLIE: No.

TED: No she doesn't? Or no it's not true?

CHARLIE: She wears underwear, Ted.

BONNY: Of course she does.

TED: How do you know, Charlie? Have you looked?

CHARLIE: Knock it off, Ted. O.K.?

BONNY: Yes, Ted. Stop teasing. Really.
  (THEY drive.)

TED: What does she pay you, Charlie?

CHARLIE: Never mind.

BONNY: My father says it's rude to talk about money.

TED: Hey look. I'm just a poor Canuck who wants to know what the rich Americans are paying their help this summer.

CHARLIE: She's not rich.

TED: That's why she only pays a quarter.

CHARLIE: There are more things in this world than money, Ted.

BONNY: Yes, Ted.

TED: Such as what?

BONNY: Look out for that car!
  (TED swerves. They all lean. TED straightens the "wheel.")

CHARLIE: Jesus. Drive much?

TED: I saw him.

CHARLIE: Uh huh. You betchum, Ted.

TED: I want to know what the Pig Woman gives you that's more important than money, Charlie.

CHARLIE: Things you wouldn't understand, Ted.

TED: Such as what? *(Silence from Charlie)*

BONNY: Such as what, Charlie?

CHARLIE: Whose side are you on, Bonny?

BONNY: I'm just curious, Charlie. What does she give you?

CHARLIE: She . . . teaches me things.

TED: *Teaches* you? You mean, like a . . . *teacher*?

BONNY: What does she teach you, Charlie?

CHARLIE: She . . . I don't have to tell.

TED: You don't have to ride the Cyclone, either. *(HE stops the "car." They all jerk forward.)* Maybe we'll just sit here by the side of the road until we hear about those wonderful, secret, piggy things.

BONNY: Oh, Ted.

CHARLIE: Fine with me. Maybe there are more important things than riding some dumb machine in an amusement park.

BONNY: Oh, Charlie.

TED: O.K. We sit.

CHARLIE: You know what amusement parks are, don't you? Amusement parks are places where people fritter away their potential.

TED: Fritter away their what?

CHARLIE: Potential. Potential.

BONNY: What does that mean, Charlie?

CHARLIE: It means that everyone's got his potential, if they only use it right. I've got it, you've got it, Hitler's got it, even Ted's got it.

BONNY: Is that what she teaches you, Charlie?

CHARLIE: Sure. And she's trying to bring mine out.

TED: Yeah well tell her I got some potential right here in my pants.

BONNY: That's disgusting, Ted.

CHARLIE: Yes, Ted. Knock it off. There are ladies present.

TED: Want to make something out of it, Charlie?

BONNY: Oh stop!

TED: Or don't you have enough potential?

CHARLIE: I'll make something out of it, Ted.

TED: O.K., then let's get out of the car, you dumb little creep.

CHARLIE: *(Pushing against Bonny's seat)* O.K., you crude Canadian townie hick!

TED: *(Leaping out of the "car")* You'll be gumming your food, buster!

BONNY: Oh God!

CHARLIE: *(Holding his ground)* I'm not scared of you!
(THEY square off. BONNY is out of the "car" by now, and comes between them.)

BONNY: Oh stop! Please! Ted, you're two years older!

CHARLIE: Just a year and a half.
(THEY face each other. Then TED backs off.)

TED: You're lucky there's a woman around, Charlie.

CHARLIE: *(Making his knees shake, like a cartoon character)* I'm scared, Ted. Help. Gasp. Shriek.
(HE starts Off L.)

BONNY: How will you get home, Charlie?

CHARLIE: Who has to go home? I've got other places to go besides home!
(HE runs Off. BONNY returns to the "car." TED tries to close the "door" for her. SHE slams it shut herself.)

TED: *(To BONNY; through the "window")* Still want to go to the Cyclone?

BONNY: I don't know . . .
(TED moodily gets into the "car." ELSIE comes out with her book, settles D.L. in chair to read.)

TED: Or do you want to just sit out here, in the middle of nowhere?

BONNY: Maybe you'd better take me, back, Ted.

TED: Knew it. Home to Daddy, eh?

(THEY drive. BONNY looks out the window. TED turns on the "car radio." Music comes up: a wartime song like "Praise the Lord and Pass the Ammunition." GRACE comes out from U.L., carrying sweater and purse. SHE comes D. to comb hair, as if in a "mirror.")

ELSIE: Where are you going?

GRACE: Mr. McAlister very sweetly asked me to go to the movies.

ELSIE: To *Dumbo?*

GRACE: *Dumbo?* I thought it was *Now Voyager.*

ELSIE: By the way, Mrs. Blackburn called. She says the Latin situation is beyond repair.

GRACE: Oh dear. Where is he?

ELSIE: Out with the gang.

GRACE: At least it's with them.

TED: *(In "car")* Maybe I should get someone else to ride the Cyclone.

BONNY: Maybe you should.

ELSIE: *(To Grace)* You should write Daddy about him.

GRACE: I don't want to worry him.

ELSIE: But he's a *man.* He could help.

GRACE: Maybe . . .

ELSIE: If you don't write him, I will, Mother.

GRACE: Now this is *my* problem, Elsie, and I'll thank you to stay out of it. *(SHE gives her a quick kiss.)* . . . I'll write him tomorrow. I promise.

(SHE goes U.L. to stand and wait, back to audience, as if on a porch. ELSIE reads War and Peace. *Music continues underneath. ANNA and CHARLIE enter as if in moonlight.)*

ANNA: When does she want you home? What's the rule?

CHARLIE: Eleven.

ANNA: All right. Then we have a choice. We can sit out here and study the stars, or we can go inside, and read selections from the poetry of William Butler Yeats. Maybe you're an astronomer. Or a poet. Which will it be?

CHARLIE: Let me think . . .

ANNA: Now remember. It's a choice, and at your age, all choices are important. They tell you who you are. So which is it?

CHARLIE: Um . . .

(HE stands thinking, ANNA looking at lake. The Lights focus down on CHARLIE's face. The music continues.)

END OF ACT ONE

ACT TWO

Before Curtain: Music: another old Bing Crosby recording, such as "Accentuate the Positive." CHARLIE comes On hurriedly from R.

CHARLIE: This is still a play about me, when I was fourteen—
(ANNA crosses UP, from L. to R. carrying a bushel basket.)

ANNA: Come on, help me pick the peas, and then I'll show you how to put them up.

CHARLIE: *(Following her)* I have to leave early today, Anna.

ANNA: Early? Why?

CHARLIE: We're going to a party.

ANNA: *(As they cross)* What party? Tell me about this party.

CHARLIE: Well, you see, my mother thinks it would be good for me if . . .
(THEY are Off, as GRACE comes On from U.L., hurriedly, in a bathrobe.)

GRACE: *(Calling toward Off L.)* Charlie! I'm in your bathroom! And I found Daddy's old razor! Now full speed ahead!
(ELSIE comes on from U.L., also in a bathrobe.)

ELSIE: Mother, I don't have anything to wear.

GRACE: Why not your little blue Lanz?

ELSIE: It makes me look fat, Mother!

GRACE: Now is that the dress's fault? Or is that somebody else's?

ELSIE: Oh, Mothurrr . . .
(SHE goes Off. GRACE speaks to audience.)

GRACE: *(To audience)* Here's what's happening. We're all going to a party. The Ralph Wheelers are giving a big shindig for their daughter, Sylvia. It will be out at Prospect Point, and they plan to have music, and dancing, and the works, just like before the war. I'm thrilled. I'm absolutely delighted. It will get Charlie away from that woman, and Elsie away from her book, and me away from *myself*, at least for a while . . .

(ELSIE comes back on from U.L.)

ELSIE: Are you sure Charlie's invited, Mother?

GRACE: Absolutely. I called up and asked.

ELSIE: You mean, you wangled an invitation?

GRACE: I had to, Elsie.

ELSIE: But he'll be *out* of it, Mother. They all go away to school.

GRACE: That's the point, Elsie. I am thinking of the fall.

ELSIE: Oh. Right. I forgot . . . *(Ominously)* The fall.

(SHE hurries Off, U.L.)

GRACE: *(To audience)* Which needs explaining. Guess what arrived from the Pacific last week. A great stack of letters. For all of us! Oh he's fine! He's alive, and well, and frantic to come home, though he thinks we've got a while before the Japanese surrender. *(Takes airmail letter out of the pocket of her robe)* But this is the crucial one. This he wrote in response to my S.O.S. about Charlie. Listen: *(SHE opens it, reads.)* ". . . Sounds to me as if the boy should go right off to boarding school. Sounds as if he's lost his bearings. I was sent to Saint Luke's when I was fifteen, and it shaped me right up. Send him away." *(SHE folds the letter.)* So guess who's been on the long-distance telephone. I called Saint Luke's, and I called George Graham in Philadelphia, who's on the board of trustees, and I called Sam Satterfield in Greenwich, who gives them scads of money—I alerted the whole network. And what with one thing and another, the school's going to take him. Latin or no Latin, in September. Off he goes, if we can just hold on till then! *(Calls Off)* Charlie!

(CHARLIE comes out from U.L., *in boxer shorts and socks.)*

CHARLIE: Do I have to go to the party?

GRACE: Of course you do. Now here's the razor. Have you any idea how to use it?

CHARLIE: I used to watch Dad.

GRACE: Then let's see if you can end up looking halfway presentable for the Wheelers.

CHARLIE: *(Mixing "lather" in front of "mirror")* Who's Saliva Wheeler anyway?

GRACE: Her name is Sylvia! And she's very attractive, and if you don't dance with her at least once, I'm going to personally throttle you.

(GRACE goes Off, U.L. *CHARLIE begins to "shave" meticulously, facing front, as if in a mirror. ANNA comes On* D.R. *with her bushel basket, settles down to shelling "peas.")*

CHARLIE: I have to go, Anna.

ANNA: Good. Go, then. You'll learn something. I used to go myself. Years ago, when my family had money. Oh sure. I was on the list. I went. I came out. I wore white. I carried flowers. Yellow roses and baby's breath. I danced. I was the belle of the ball. Can you imagine? Me? Anna Trumbull, the Pig Woman, dancing till dawn? . . . I didn't enjoy it, though. I saw too much. I saw into the kitchen and under the rug. I gave it up. But you go. Look them over. Then you'll know what you're up against.

CHARLIE: *(Into "mirror)* I won't know anybody. I don't even know the Wheelers.

ANNA: *(Shelling peas)* I do. Ralph Wheeler's father was on the way up while mine was on the way down. We'd nod to each other on Delaware Avenue, like freighters passing on the lake. Of course, their money is absolutely corrupt. Behind every great fortune is a great crime. Theirs was killing horses. When the automobile came in, old Walt

Wheeler, who ran a livery stable down on Richmond Avenue, simply bought up every horse he could get his hands on. Dirt cheap. And then he systematically took them out behind the barn and cut their throats.

CHARLIE: *("Nicking" his neck)* Ouch!

ANNA: He sold the hides to the shoe people, the hooves to the glue people, the hair to the mattress people, and the meat, at outrageous prices, to the poor immigrants who were coming in to break their backs for Lackawanna Steel. And with his profits, he built his place out here. So when you get there, just remember: the whole shebang is built on the bones of dead horses!

(GRACE comes into the "bathroom" from U.L. SHE carries a seersucker jacket, clean khakis, a striped tie, a blue Oxford-cloth button-down shirt for CHARLIE and a pair of loafers.)

GRACE: I got out your suit. And here's a tie. And I ironed your shirt for you. And polished these.

(SHE lays them out on the glider.)

You can always tell a gentlemen by his linen and his leather.

(SHE goes Off L.)

CHARLIE: *(Into "mirror")* A lot of snooty boarding school kids will be there.

ANNA: *(Shelling "peas")* Good. Now they've decided to ship you off, you should meet your fellow prisoners. The boarding school crowd. I knew them, too. I remember the Watson boy. He was the one who ran away from Hotchkiss. He was happy at Deerfield, though. Once he was hit on the head by a hockey puck, he fell right into line . . .

(ELSIE comes On from L., now dressed for the party. SHE comes D.L., as if she were now in GRACE's bedroom, standing in front of a full-length mirror.)

ELSIE: *(Calling Off)* Mother, I'm borrowing your lipstick, please.

(SHE puts on lipstick in the "mirror." CHARLIE, Center, has finished shaving, and is putting on his clothes.)

CHARLIE: And a lot of superficial girls . . .

ANNA: And then there was the Patterson girl. She was seduced by her riding master at finishing school. They never taught her how to cross her legs.

(GRACE comes On from L., crosses D.L. into her "bedroom," now dressed for the party. SHE and ELSIE straighten their seams, and put on makeup in front of the "mirror." CHARLIE continues to dress.)

ELSIE: Do I have too much lipstick on, Mother?

GRACE: It never hurts to have less, dear.

ELSIE: I won't have anyone to dance with.

GRACE: You'd be surprised. All the boys are beginning to come home.

ELSIE: But I won't know any of them.

GRACE: All the better. You might find yourself dancing with Prince Andrei Bolkonski.

ELSIE: *(Looking at her)* When did you read *War and Peace,* Mother?

GRACE: Oh heavens . . . before I was married I read a lot . . . Now powder your nose, and get your hair out of your eyes. *(Calling toward CHARLIE)* Charlie, come into my room, please. I want to see how you've done.

CHARLIE: *(Dressed by now)* So I gotta go, Anna.

ANNA: Sure. Fine. Go. While you're there, say hello to Bill McMartin. He built a chemical factory right on the lake. Whenever I see a dead fish, I think of Bill.

(CHARLIE crosses D.L. into GRACE's area.)

GRACE: Well look at you! Charlie, I think tonight I'm going to break down and let you have a glass of beer. After all, you're almost fifteen.

ANNA: You'll have to drink, of course. It makes them easier to tolerate. That's how I got hooked on the old firewater.

GRACE: *(To Charlie)* Now come here, and let's see if we all pass inspection.

(SHE stands between CHARLIE and ELSIE, as if they were all in front of a full-length mirror. SHE puts her arms around her children.)

There. Oh, I wish someone were here to take our picture.

ELSIE: And send it to Daddy.

GRACE: Yes. I happen to think we look very snappy. Except for your tie, Charlie.

CHARLIE: What's wrong with my tie?

GRACE: It's all over the place, my friend. Here. Let me fuss with it.

(SHE undoes Charlie's tie, starts tying it again.)

CHARLIE: Ouch.

GRACE: Hold still.

CHARLIE: *(As GRACE struggles with his tie)* PLEASE, Mom.

GRACE: Just hold still.

ANNA: *(Gathering up her bushel basket)* Yes, well, go on. Go to the party. Wear their uniform, drink their liquor, learn their dance steps. Maybe you'll like it. Maybe that's your potential, after all.

(SHE goes Off R. as CHARLIE suddenly pulls away from GRACE.)

CHARLIE: Lay off, Mom! You're *strangling* me!

GRACE: I'm just trying to get it straight.

CHARLIE: *(Ripping off the tie, throwing it down)* I'm not wearing this tie!

GRACE: Pick that up.

CHARLIE: Make me. *(Pause)*

ELSIE: Uh oh.

GRACE: That is your father's necktie.

CHARLIE: I don't care. *(Pause)*

GRACE: We are late for the party.

CHARLIE: I don't want to go.

ELSIE: Oh Lord. *(Pause)*

GRACE: Come on, then, Elsie. We'll go without him.

CHARLIE: I don't give a shit.

GRACE: *(Wheeling on him)* I ought to wash your mouth out with soap!

CHARLIE: I don't give a flying fuck.

ELSIE: Oh my God!

(GRACE hauls off and lets him have it, slapping him across the face, hard. Long pause.)

CHARLIE: *(Grimly)* O.K., Mom! This is IT! *(HE rips off his jacket, throws it down on the ground.)* No more parties for me! *(Rips off his shirt)* Never again! I never want to see those people! Ever! *(Rips off his pants)* I don't want to talk to them . . . *(Throws off a shoe)* I don't want to be with them . . . *(Throws off the other shoe, and his socks)* I don't want to dance on the bones of dead horses! *(HE is now in his undershorts.)*

GRACE: What are you talking about?

CHARLIE: I don't want to go away to school, either! I don't want to go to *any* school, ever again! I want to stay out here, all year round! With Anna! I want to live in her barn, and eat her tomatoes, and realize my potential any time I want! And you know what I want to do now? I want to go down to the lake and dive under the water and get clean, really clean, CLEAN.

(HE runs Offstage, his underpants fly back Onstage. Long pause.)

GRACE: *(Quietly; to Elsie)* Go see what he does, please.

(ELSIE exits quickly. GRACE goes around the stage, quickly picking up CHARLIE's scattered clothes. She sits down, gathering them all in her lap. She notices her husband's tie and smooths it out as best she can. ELSIE comes back in.)

Well? What?

ELSIE: He ran right down the steps and into the water.

GRACE: I'm sure.

ELSIE: Stark naked. While it's still light out. And Mrs. Wilson was strolling on the beach! With her sister-in-law! Who's Catholic!

GRACE: I'm sure.

ELSIE: And I'll bet when he comes out, he heads straight for the Pig Woman, Mother. I'll bet he does.

GRACE: I imagine.

ELSIE: So what'll we do, Mother? What'll we do now?

GRACE: Do? I'll tell you what we'll do. We'll go to the party, that's what we'll do. And we'll have a perfectly spectacular time. *(SHE stands up.)* We'll drink too much, and eat too much, and kiss every man in sight! And when we're good and loaded, we might just sneak up on old Mrs. Stockwell, and push her into the pool! And if people ask us about Charlie, we'll say, "Who's he? We don't know any Charlie. All we know is that the night is young, and we are beautiful, and we're raring to go!" And then tomorrow morning, bright and early—no, not bright and early, but at a convenient hour—I'll tell you what else I'm going to do! I'm going to make a visit! The Shadow here is going to pay one hell of a call on the Pig Woman! Meanwhile, let's move it, sister! Let's shake a leg! We are going to live it up, if it kills us!

(GRACE strides out U.L. ELSIE stands, amazed, and then trots after her, as the light changes to early evening. ANNA comes out from U.R., carrying a greasy kerosene lamp, a dusty bottle of wine, and two old cups. SHE puts down the lantern, pours herself some wine, and sits contemplatively. CHARLIE comes On from R.)

ANNA: I thought you were going to catch us our breakfast.

CHARLIE: It's getting too dark to fish.

ANNA: Nonsense. Try again.

CHARLIE: *(Hesitating)* Why hasn't she come yet?

ANNA: She will.

CHARLIE: Maybe she won't. Maybe she's so mad at me, she's just given up.

ANNA: Oh no. She'll be here. After all, this is the perfect time for a powwow: The witching hour . . . the children's hour . . . lately what's known in town as the cocktail hour. This is when she'll come. First let her get the casserole in the oven. And wash the lettuce. And comb her hair. Then she'll be on her way.

CHARLIE: You sure know my mom.

ANNA: I know her very well. She'll park her car down by the barn. She'll sit for a moment, organizing her thoughts. Then she'll get out, and start up the path. She'll come to the fork by the old elm. Will she take the short cut? No, she will not. Little Red Riding Hood will take the long way around. She'll pass the outhouse, circle the rhubarb, notice our light, take a deep breath, and call . . .

GRACE: *(From Off* L.*)* ANNA!

CHARLIE: Golly, Anna. You're amazing.

ANNA: *(To Charlie)* You see? Now *fish!* You promised.
   (CHARLIE goes Off D.R. *to fish.)*

GRACE: *(Off* L., *closer)* Anna?

ANNA: *(Calling Off)* Out here.
   (GRACE comes On briskly. THEY look at each other. GRACE holds out her hand. ANNA holds up her hand, in mock Indian fashion.)
   How.
   (A moment. Then GRACE laughs.)

GRACE: Oh, Anna.
   (THEY shake hands.)

ANNA: Long time, no see.

GRACE: I know it.

ANNA: Twenty years.

GRACE: Oh, not *twenty* . . .

ANNA: Twenty. Almost exactly.

GRACE: Mercy. Has it been that long? Well I mean, we've *seen* each other, haven't we? Occasionally. We've seen each other . . .

ANNA: You had talent twenty years ago.

GRACE: Don't be silly.

ANNA: You had potential.

GRACE: Oh please . . . *(Pause)*

ANNA: Well. You're looking for the boy.

GRACE: Yes, actually.

ANNA: He's down fishing off the rocks.

GRACE: How nice. *(Pause)* I assume he spent last night here.

ANNA: In the barn.

GRACE: He didn't even have a toothbrush.

ANNA: He didn't need one.

GRACE: Well, I imagine he needs one now. And is ready for his own bed.

ANNA: No.

GRACE: No?

ANNA: No. *(Pause)* Want a drink?

GRACE: Oh heavens no.

ANNA: Have a taste of the local wine.

GRACE: Local? Do the Canadians make wine?

ANNA: I do.

GRACE: Anna, you were always so resourceful . . .

ANNA: The house wine, then? *(SHE pours a cup.)*

GRACE: Why that sounds very nice, actually.

ANNA: Here you are. *(Hands her a cup and pours another for herself)*

GRACE: *(Sipping)* Mmmm.

ANNA: You like it?

GRACE: Oh yes.

ANNA: You don't. But we'll pretend you do.

GRACE: Anna . . .

ANNA: *(Producing a strange, ratty, multicolored patch of knitting from her pocket)* Look at this.

GRACE: *(Taking it)* What is it?

ANNA: We've been working with wool.

GRACE: Oh.

ANNA: What do you think?

GRACE: Looks a little . . . tangled, Anna.

ANNA: That's the point.

GRACE: The point?

ANNA: That's what he's trying to say.

GRACE: Look, Anna, don't you think if he had any real talent, we would have noticed it?

ANNA: No.

GRACE: Then don't you think someone at school, someone at camp might have pointed it out?

ANNA: No.

GRACE: But he's never shown the slightest interest!

ANNA: Until now.

GRACE: All right, then. Fine, Anna. Thank you. Thank you for taking him under your wing. He's had a good experience. I appreciate it. Thank you.

ANNA: You're welcome.

GRACE: But he's not the world's next Michelangelo, Anna, and he has to continue his education, and I'd appreciate it very much if you'd tell him that.

ANNA: Tell him yourself.

GRACE: I have, Anna. Of course. And I will again. But I'm afraid at this point he listens more to you.

ANNA: He won't listen to me if I tell him that.

(GRACE puts down her cup.)

GRACE: All right now, Anna, let's be frank.

ANNA: You don't like my wine.

GRACE: No I don't, Anna. And I don't like what you're doing either. And I want to know why.

ANNA: I'm a teacher, remember. He came. I'm teaching him.

GRACE: Teaching him what, for God's sake?

ANNA: What I taught you, once upon a time.

GRACE: I was a poor student, Anna.

ANNA: You were the best. You could have done anything. And you settled for a Still Life.

GRACE: Oh Anna, stop. Please.

ANNA: I never stop. It's against my religion. *(Pause)*

GRACE: I'd like to make a deal with you, Anna.

ANNA: I don't make deals.

GRACE: You might make this one. Suppose you let him go by the middle of August.

ANNA: Suppose I don't.

GRACE: Suppose I give you a check if you do.

ANNA: A check?

GRACE: For all you've done. For Charlie.

ANNA: A check.

GRACE: *(Starting to open her purse)* I brought along a check, Anna.

ANNA: *(Bursting into laughter)* A check! Ohboyohboyohboy! It seems to me I've heard that song before.

GRACE: I'm serious, Anna.

ANNA: *(Laughing)* Oh I know you are!

GRACE: I'm trying to find a solution here.

ANNA: Seems to me I remember another check twenty years ago.

GRACE: I don't know what you mean.

ANNA: I remember your own father showing up with a check.

GRACE: I didn't know that.

ANNA: Oh yes. Seems I was a bad influence on you, and he wanted to buy me off. And I told him just what I told you: I never stop.

GRACE: I swear I didn't know that, Anna.

ANNA: Oh yes. And when I refused the check, he said he'd see to it that I stopped. And he did! But not before his daughter landed on my doorstep in the middle of the night.

GRACE: I knew we'd get to this . . .

ANNA: You ran straight to me a week before your wedding!

GRACE: I had a slight case of cold feet . . .

ANNA: You wanted to change your life!

GRACE: I was a confused young girl!

ANNA: You were a courageous young woman! Before your parents yanked you out of my studio, postponed the wedding, and dragged you kicking and screaming across half the continent of Europe!

GRACE: Well I'm glad they did! I'm happily married now!

ANNA: You are, eh?

GRACE: Yes I am, Anna! And I've got two wonderful children to prove it!

ANNA: Prove it? How? By shipping them off to prison? By taking your son's natural energies and stifling them, just as your parents stifled your own?

GRACE: Oh, Anna, what are we talking about? What could I do? What could I paint? A few pale peonies in a pot. And what can Charlie do? That thing, that rag you've got? And what can *you* do, Anna, really, when the chips are down? What have you ever made? When have you ever been shown? When have you ever received even the smallest signal from the outside world? Oh come on. You're a captivating teacher, and you excite the young, but this is amateur night around here, and you know it. You and Charlie have been playing in the mud, and now it's time for everyone to clean up and go home.

ANNA: Home, is it? Some home! Seems to me that while your husband has been laying down his life for that home, and while your children were fast asleep in that home, you've been sneaking down the beach to the gold star home of Bob McAlister. *(Pause)*

GRACE: That's vicious and vindictive and cruel!

ANNA: Yes, well, look who else has been playing in the mud.

GRACE: Who told you?

ANNA: I'm the Pig Woman, remember. I'm good at rooting around. *(Pause)*

GRACE: Does Charlie know?

ANNA: No.

GRACE: Will you tell him?

ANNA: No.

GRACE: Thank you. *(Sits on glider)* It's over anyway. It was a small thing at a bad time and I regret it more than you know.

ANNA: All I know is that you were a woman of pride and promise, and you chose a shadow of a life when you left me!

GRACE: Oh, Anna! Please! No more! No more! *(Pause)* It's been such a lonely summer.

ANNA: Welcome to the club.

GRACE: Did my father really stop you from teaching?

ANNA: Oh not directly. He simply told all the other fathers how dangerous I was. Somehow, my students stopped showing up.

GRACE: I'm sorry.

ANNA: And for some reason, I heard nothing more from you.

GRACE: I got married, Anna. I had babies . . .

ANNA: Oh well. Doc Holloway set me up out here. One thing about men: they put their wagons in a circle, but there's always one who's willing to sneak out after dark. *(Pointedly)* As you also seem to have discovered, recently. *(Pause)*

GRACE: Oh, Anna, I'm hanging on by my fingernails.

ANNA: *(Holding her cup of wine)* Try this. It helps.

GRACE: *(Sipping her wine)* It's not bad, after all.

ANNA: See what you've been missing? (SHE *sits down beside her.*)

GRACE: I've missed *you*, Anna. I admit it. Over the years. Many times, when things have gotten me down, I've wanted to come over. Just to see you.

ANNA: I've been here.

GRACE: Lately I've been wondering what I'd be like if I'd taken the other road.

ANNA: Now's the time to find out.

GRACE: Oh God, it's a little late for that.

ANNA: Not for him.

GRACE: You mean Charlie.

ANNA: That's who I mean.

GRACE: *(Gets up, crosses* D.R.*)* You see, Anna, what you do? . . . I'd almost forgotten Charlie.

ANNA: I haven't . . . Let him stay.

GRACE: For how long?

ANNA: As long as he wants. *(Pause)*

GRACE: He could decide to stay all winter.

ANNA: He could.

GRACE: Knowing Charlie . . . Knowing you . . .

ANNA: He could.

GRACE: Away from town. Away from school.

ANNA: Why not?

GRACE: He'd fall behind, Anna!

ANNA: Behind what? *(No answer)* Hmmm? Behind what?

GRACE: I want him home, Anna.

ANNA: The old story, eh?

GRACE: I want him home.

  (ANNA *gets up.*)

ANNA: That's it, then.

GRACE: Yes.

ANNA: I'm beginning to hear drums. In Indian territory.

GRACE: I think I'd like to see him now.

ANNA: You know what he looks like.

GRACE: I'd like to talk to my own son, please.

ANNA: You've talked to him all his life.

GRACE: *(Calling out)* Charlie!

ANNA: He's too far away.

GRACE: Then I'll get him. *(SHE starts Off* R.*)*

ANNA: See if he'll come.

GRACE: *(Stopping, turning)* I could call the police, Anna.

ANNA: Much good they'd do.

GRACE: They'd bring him home.

ANNA: And he'd run away. *(Pause)*

GRACE: All right then, Anna. Let him choose. But let it be a fair choice. I'll have to trust you on that. And I'll have to trust myself. Trust all we've done in bringing him up. I don't think I've lived a shadow of a life, Anna. I love my family, and I've worked hard, and I'm proud of what I've done. And if I had to choose again, I'd choose this. And I think Charlie will, too! Blood is thicker than water, after all. Or mud.

ANNA: We'll see.

GRACE: Yes. Well I'll trust that it is.

ANNA: I'll trust him.

GRACE: *(Looking at her watch)* Mercy. Look at the time. It's getting late.

ANNA: Yes.

GRACE: I've got a casserole in the oven.

ANNA: I'm sure.

ANNA: I imagine he'd like some. It's his favorite thing.

ANNA: He's already eaten.

GRACE: That never seemed to make much difference.

ANNA: Let him fish.

GRACE: Let him choose, Anna. That's the deal. Tell him we're having shepherd's pie.

ANNA: Why don't you trot out your left breast, and bribe him with that? *(Pause)*

GRACE: *(Grimly)* Good night, Anna.

(SHE *turns and goes Off* L. ANNA *takes a long slug of wine.* CHARLIE *comes On with his fishing rod, hurriedly.)*

CHARLIE: Was that her car?

ANNA: Yes.

CHARLIE: Did she go?

ANNA: Yes.

CHARLIE: Already?

ANNA: Yes.

CHARLIE: Was she sore at me?

ANNA: No.

CHARLIE: Does she want me back?

ANNA: Yes.

CHARLIE: Do you think I should . . . touch base?

ANNA: Touch base?

CHARLIE: See her. Say hello. Do you think I should?

ANNA: It's up to you. *(Pause)*

CHARLIE: Maybe I better.

(*HE starts off toward where* GRACE *has gone.*)

ANNA: Charlie . . . (*HE stops. This is tough for her.*) I've decided to let you work on my car.

CHARLIE: Hey! When?

ANNA: Any time you want.

CHARLIE: Now?

ANNA: Here. Take the light.

(*CHARLIE takes the lantern and runs Off* R. ANNA *takes her wine bottle and cups, and goes off behind him.* BONNY *comes on from* U.L. *She speaks to the audience.*)

BONNY: You know where this is? This is the place out on the back road where Charlie and Ted and I used to sell lemonade in the old days. I got a secret note from Charlie, asking me to meet him here, so here I am. *(Looks around)* I shouldn't even be here. My parents would kill me if they knew. They think he's bad news from the word go. My mother thinks he's worse than Ted, even. So I had to lie to them. I told them I was going over to Janice's to listen to the "Hit Parade." Oh God, I'm lying more and more! Is this what it means to become a woman? And why is it we women are always drawn to such dangerous men? I feel like Juliet, in Shakespeare's play of the same name. Who says this whole thing isn't secretly about me? *(SHE shivers.)* What a scary place this is, at night. Right around here is where Margie Matthews met that skunk. And here's where the Harveys' dachshund named Pickle was run over by the milkman. If I had any sense, I'd go over to Janice's after all. Anything, but stand around and wait for a crazy boy who's run away from his own home! But I can't let him down. Maybe the Pig Woman isn't feeding him properly. Or maybe she's keeping him in sexual bondage. Whatever that means. I've got to stay. It's my duty as a friend and neighbor. *(From Offstage, a flash of headlights, and the sound of an old car horn: A-hoo-ga.)* Oh help! What's that? Maybe it's some of those fresh Canadian boys out in the car, drinking Molson's ale! *(SHE starts to hide. CHARLIE comes On from U.L.)*

CHARLIE: Hey. It's me. *(HE looks all slicked up for a date.)*

BONNY: Charlie!

CHARLIE: *(Dangling a set of car keys)* And look what comes with me.

BONNY: A car?

CHARLIE: A 1932 Reo. It's Anna's.

BONNY: Did you steal it?

CHARLIE: Hell no. I got it started. So she's letting me drive it.

BONNY: Without a license?

CHARLIE: Licenses are simply the way the bureaucrats keep themselves in power.

BONNY: Do you like living with her, Charlie?

CHARLIE: Oh sure.

BONNY: Is she . . . your mistress?

CHARLIE: Naw. I sleep in the barn.

BONNY: Don't you ever see your mother?

CHARLIE: Oh sure. I stop by. Now and then. To pick up my laundry.

BONNY: What does she say?

CHARLIE: Oh she begs me to come home. A couple of times she even cried a little.

BONNY: It's hard to imagine your mother crying.

CHARLIE: Well she did. Yesterday, in fact. So I had to hang around for a while. And then Anna got all itchy when I was late. That's when she said I could drive the car.

BONNY: Oh, Charlie, you've got two grown women fighting over you, tooth and nail!

CHARLIE: I know it . . . come on. I'll take you for a spin.

BONNY: I'm not supposed to go near you, Charlie.

CHARLIE: Come on. We'll ride the Cyclone.

BONNY: The Cyclone?

CHARLIE: Why not? We'll stop by for Ted, and make him sit in the rumble seat.

BONNY: Ted's already been on the Cyclone.

CHARLIE: No kidding? When?

BONNY: Last week. He took that girl with the big chest who serves double-dips at Brodie's.

CHARLIE: That horny bastard. O.K. We go by ourselves.

BONNY: But how will we get on? We're not sixteen.

CHARLIE: That's easy. When they ask, I'll just wave these car keys under their nose.

BONNY: But will that work?

CHARLIE: Sure. Listen, Bonny, one thing I've learned around here this summer. One thing I've learned. You're sixteen, if you feel sixteen. And if you feel sixteen, you act sixteen. And when you act sixteen, people treat you like sixteen. That's what I've learned.

BONNY: How true.

CHARLIE: So come on. Let's make our move.

BONNY: My father would kill me if he knew I was riding in a car with a boy.

CHARLIE: You're not. You're riding with a man. Now come on! Let's go!

(HE goes Off L. SHE follows. The stage goes dark. Immediately, there is the sound of a telephone ringing, stridently. It is picked up in the middle of a ring. A small light comes up, as ELSIE comes On from L. in her pajamas, rubbing her eyes.)

ELSIE: *(Calling toward R.)* Mother? . . . Who is it, Mother? Is it about . . . Daddy? *(To audience)* Oh I know it is. This is the way it happens. Everyone's sound asleep, and then suddenly the telephone rings, and—

(GRACE comes On from R. in her bathrobe, dazed.)

GRACE: That was about Charlie.

ELSIE: Charlie?

GRACE: He's had an auto accident. Bonny was with him. Nobody's dead, thank God.

ELSIE: How could he possibly . . . ?

GRACE: He was driving Anna's car, and ran right smack into a stone wall.

ELSIE: Oh Lord.

GRACE: The police said they're lucky they weren't killed. *(SHE leans on the back of the chair.)* Oh I give up, Elsie. I've had it. I have no idea what to do.

ELSIE: Do? Well the first thing we do is go see him, Mother. Where is he?

GRACE: I think they said Fort Erie.

ELSIE: Fort Erie hospital? Is he there?

GRACE: I don't even know where it is.

ELSIE: Then we find it, Mother. We get dressed, and drive to Fort Erie, and ask.

GRACE: I couldn't drive. Not in a million years.

ELSIE: Mother. Come *on!* Pull yourself together! Get dressed, and while you're doing that, I'll call Doctor Burke, and ask him where the hospital is, and he can *meet* us there, and I'll even *drive*, Mother.

GRACE: *(Looking at her)* You will?

ELSIE: Yes I will. Now go on, Mother! Hurry! Make tracks!

GRACE: Oh, thank you, Elsie.

(SHE hurries Off R. ELSIE turns to the audience.)

ELSIE: Good God! Maybe this play *is* about me, after all.

(SHE hurries out L., as the Lights come up, bright, as if on the sunroom of a hospital. TED comes On from R. dressed for a visit. He carries a package, crudely wrapped in brown paper. CHARLIE comes On from L., wearing a neck brace.)

TED: Well, well.

CHARLIE: *(Gloomily)* Hi, Ted.

TED: *(Looking around)* Nice sun room they have here. Nice and sunny.

CHARLIE: Yeah well.

TED: *(Handing him the package)* I brought you some reading material.

CHARLIE: *(Taking it)* Thanks.

TED: Open it.

(CHARLIE sits and opens it diffidently. It is a stack of old comic books.)

My permanent collection. Everything's there: the double issue of Hawkman, Mandrake meets the Phantom, everything . . .

CHARLIE: Thanks.

TED: That thing on your neck, you look like Prince Valiant, in armor.

CHARLIE: I'm supposed to be glad it's not broken.

TED: I just saw Bonny.

CHARLIE: Yeah?

TED: She's going home today.

CHARLIE: The nurse told me.

TED: Her old man was there, helping with her stuff.

CHARLIE: Oh God.

TED: She looks fine. They say she'll have just a tiny scar on her cheek. Like a permanent dimple.

CHARLIE: Is she sore at me?

TED: Naw.

CHARLIE: I'll bet she's sore.

TED: She said she wished she could have visited with you.

CHARLIE: I didn't feel like it. O.K.?

TED: O.K. *(Pause)*

CHARLIE: Her old man's sore at me, isn't he?

TED: Naw.

CHARLIE: I'll bet he's gunning for me.

TED: Naw. He's gunning for the Pig Woman. He said it was her fault for giving you the car, and he's going to sue the pants off her.

CHARLIE: Oh jeez . . .

TED: I said she didn't wear any pants . . . Was I right?

CHARLIE: I wrecked her car, you know. They're selling it for junk.

TED: Next time remember to hit the brakes.

CHARLIE: I did, goddammit! They broke. Even the police said that.

TED: O.K. O.K. *(Pause)* Want to read comics?

CHARLIE: Maybe later.

TED: There's a new one, where they bring in a Batgirl.

CHARLIE: I'll get 'em back to you, Ted.

TED: No, keep 'em. I got to give 'em up. We're moving.

CHARLIE: Moving? How come?

TED: My dad took a job in Toronto. He says after the war, Toronto is going up and Buffalo is going down.

CHARLIE: Bullshit.

TED: That's what he says. He says Canada's going to be a great nation, and we're getting in on the ground floor.

CHARLIE: Ho hum. Snore snore. Wake me when you're finished, O.K.?

TED: Yeah well I'm going to technical school and learn about electronics.

CHARLIE: Next summer tell me all about it

TED: I won't be around next summer, Charlie. That's what I'm telling you. *(Pause)*

CHARLIE: Oh.

TED: So when you read those comics, think of me, O.K.?

CHARLIE: O.K. I will, Ted.

(Pause. BONNY comes on from R.)

BONNY: Hi, Charlie.

(CHARLIE looks away from her, sheepishly.)

TED: He's really sick. He doesn't feel like reading comics.

BONNY: I told my father I wouldn't leave until I could see you, Charlie. I put my foot down. *(CHARLIE can't answer.)*

TED: Don't you think he looks like Prince Valiant? Or maybe it's Chester the Turtle?

BONNY: Ted, there's a cafeteria down below, where you can get Cokes. Why don't you get us Cokes? I'll pay you back, I swear.

TED: *(Looking from one to the other; saluting)* Roger, Wilco, over and out. *(HE goes off R.)*

BONNY: Oh, Charlie!

(She sits down next to him.)

CHARLIE: I could of killed you.

BONNY: Oh don't be silly. As the doctor said, we were young. We bounced.

CHARLIE: I'll never drive a car again.

BONNY: Now, now . . .

CHARLIE: Never! I'll never drive. I'll never go out with girls, I'll never fall in love, I'll never get married . . .

BONNY: Oh gee . . .

CHARLIE: I'm a goner. I'm a chump. I'm just a dumb juvenile jerk. I'm a creep. I'm a weird, twerpy, stupid, fairy, pipsqueak slob of a son of BITCH!

BONNY: Charlie, stop! *(SHE kisses him impulsively. Almost at the same time, a loud church bell starts to ring energetically somewhere. They look at each other.)* What was that?

CHARLIE: I dunno.

(HE kisses her. More bells, buzzers, alarms, horns ring out, louder and louder. TED rushes in.)

TED: Hey! Guess what? The Japs have just surrendered! They gave UP! The war's over! Come on! There's a big party down in the cafeteria!

(HE runs Off. CHARLIE and BONNY follow, as the sound of horns, bells, gongs, whistles, everything comes up louder and louder, and GRACE comes out from L., now wearing a sweater. SHE speaks to the audience.)

GRACE: Well, it's the day after Labor Day, and time for everyone to move in. Already, there's a north wind whipping across the tennis courts, and the lake looks gray and shivery, and we've been using two blankets at night. It's time to get back to town.

(ELSIE comes out from L.)

Did you turn off the water?

ELSIE: Charlie's doing it.

GRACE: Then I'd better check.

ELSIE: *(To audience as SHE stacks the stool on the chair)* We've got a million things to do in town, anyway. On Tuesday, Mother takes the train to San Francisco to meet Daddy, and on Thursday, it's my responsibility to get Charlie on the Pullman for Saint Luke's School. And Holyoke starts the following week. So we've all got to buy clothes, and sew on name-tapes, and pack trunks, and somewhere in all the confusion, I've got to write a ten-page paper on *War and Peace*.

(SHE piles the furniture to one side. GRACE comes out from L.)

GRACE: Did you hide the liquor?

ELSIE: Oh no.

GRACE: Then do it, please.

(ELSIE goes L. GRACE speaks to the audience)

As far as Anna is concerned, nobody is suing anybody, thank God. Oh, there was a lot of talk, but nothing came of it. Seems she was already in dutch with the provincial government. Hadn't paid her taxes, hadn't put in plumbing. And of course the car wasn't registered. So the accident brought everything to a head. Bonny's father made a few telephone calls to Toronto, and they lowered the boom, that's all. The poor thing couldn't pay the huge fines, so the solution was, she sell her property and get out.

(ELSIE comes out from L., *carrying an old tarpaulin.)*

ELSIE: I think this is it, Mother.

(SHE and GRACE cover the porch furniture.)

GRACE: All right. Tell Charlie to check the locks on all the doors, and put the rat poison out.

ELSIE: O.K.

(SHE goes back in L.*)*

GRACE: *(Coming* D. *speaks to the audience)* I did what I could for her. Really. I went to see her. She wouldn't even answer the door. I left her a note, telling her how sorry I was. I even enclosed a check. For the car. But I never heard a word. Nothing. Though I notice the check was cashed almost immediately. I *did* hear, through the grapevine, that there's some cousin in Niagara Falls who's willing to take her in. Thank God for that . . . But you know something: I almost hate to see her go.

(ELSIE comes out again from L., *carrying her* War and Peace.*)*

ELSIE: All set, Mother.

GRACE: *(Calling Off)* Come on, Charlie! We're waiting! *(ELSIE sits in the "car," GRACE speaks to the audience.)* I do. I don't know whether this play has been about me or not, but I know I feel sad. Oh, I suppose she shouldn't be living around here anymore. Confusing the minds of the young. I know all that. But still: It's the end of something, isn't it? And that's always sad. Or do people just feel this way in the fall?

(CHARLIE comes out, still in his neck brace, now wearing a sweater.)

Did you leave a key under the mat, dear, so Mrs. Marek can get in to clean in the spring?

CHARLIE: Uh huh.

GRACE: Well then, let's go.

ELSIE: I'll drive, Mother.

GRACE: Good for you.

ELSIE: And I cleared a place in back for Charlie.

CHARLIE: Why can't I sit in front?

GRACE: Please, dear. It's easier for Elsie.

> *(They get into the "car"; CHARLIE climbs into the back, ELSIE starts the "car" jerkily.)*

ELSIE: Goodbye, house.

GRACE: Yes. You've given us quite a summer.

ELSIE: Just think. Next summer Daddy will be out here.

GRACE: I know . . . We'll all have to toe the mark, won't we?

ELSIE: *(As they "drive")* Next year, I hear they're redoing the tennis court.

GRACE: Yes. We'll be playing on a hard surface.

ELSIE: And they're building a ramp. For motor boats.

GRACE: Yes . . .

CHARLIE: Turn here . . .

ELSIE: Oh no!

GRACE: Charlie . . .

CHARLIE: Turn HERE!

GRACE: Charlie, she won't see anyone. She's been very difficult.

CHARLIE: Stop the car.

ELSIE: We're behind schedule.

CHARLIE: STOP THE CAR, or I'm jumping OUT!

GRACE: Stop the car, Elsie.

ELSIE: All right, Mother.

> *(They stop. CHARLIE gets out of the "car," crosses around to D.L.)*

GRACE: Don't be too long, dear. Please.

ELSIE: *(Grabbing her book)* Might as well start *War and Peace* all over again.

GRACE: *(Anxiously watching Charlie)* Let's hope he's not *that* long. (CHARLIE *calls out from* D.L.)

CHARLIE: Anna? *(No answer)* Anna! *(No answer)* Come on, Anna! It's just me.

(ANNA *comes out from* R. SHE *wears an old raincoat and a hat.* SHE *looks strangely suburbanized.)*

Hey, Anna. Look at you!

ANNA: Yes. Look at me. All gussied up for town. Just like one of the summer ladies.

CHARLIE: I came to apologize, Anna.

ANNA: For what? Oh you mean, for ruining my life.

CHARLIE: The brakes broke, Anna.

ANNA: So they say.

CHARLIE: Oh Anna, I'm sorry.

ANNA: Yes well, let's bury the hatchet, shall we? . . . What's that they put you in? A halter? A straightjacket?

CHARLIE: Just a neck brace. They're taking it off next week.

ANNA: Don't be too sure.

CHARLIE: Where will you be, Anna? I'll write you a letter.

ANNA: Didn't they tell you? I'm returning to my roots. I'll be living in the Tuscarora Trailer Park. Near the old Reservation.

CHARLIE: I'll come see you, Anna. Christmas vacation. I swear.

ANNA: Nonsense. The war is over. The men are coming home. Think what they'll be bringing us: New cars. Television. Jet travel. When you've got a choice between all that, and me, which will you take?

CHARLIE: You, Anna. Any day.

ANNA: Oh sure. You bet.

ELSIE: *(Calling out, impatiently)* Come on, Charlie!

GRACE: *(Restraining her)* Don't, Elsie. Give him time.

ELSIE: But what's he doing?

GRACE: Saying goodbye . . .

ANNA: *(To Charlie)* Well, the world seems to be calling you.

CHARLIE: *(Crossing to Anna)* What about my stuff?

ANNA: Your stuff?

CHARLIE: The stuff I made.

ANNA: You want it? I was going to consign it to the rubbish heap of history.

CHARLIE: I want it.

ANNA: Wait, then.

(SHE goes Off R.)

ELSIE: *(In "car")* What if he decides to stay with her again?

GRACE: He won't.

(ANNA comes out immediately from R. carrying an old cardboard box.)

ANNA: Here you are. Fragments of a lost age. *(SHE hands him the box.)* Your *oeuvre*. Your complete works.

CHARLIE: *(Taking out an inept clay object)* I never found my potential, did I?

ANNA: That's all right. I seem to have lost mine.

CHARLIE: *(Rummaging in the box)* What about my tomahtoe seeds?

ANNA: *(Automatically)* Tomaytoe seeds.

CHARLIE: You promised me some in June.

ANNA: They're in there.

(CHARLIE finds them in the box.)

CHARLIE: What about you? Aren't you keeping some?

ANNA: Where would I plant them?

CHARLIE: I don't know, Anna. Anywhere. Come on. Keep plugging. And so will I.

ANNA: Oh hell. Maybe I'll drop a few over the bones of my great-grandmother, and see what comes up.

CHARLIE: That's the ticket.

(HE shakes some seeds into her hand.)

ANNA: Well. They're picking me up any minute.

CHARLIE: *(Attempting to shake hands)* Goodbye, Anna. Thank you for a wonderful summer.

ANNA: What is this? A coming-out party?

(SHE gestures for him to bend down. HE bends stiffly over the box. SHE takes his head in her hands, and kisses him on the forehead.)

There. Now scram. I want to look at the lake.

(SHE moves D.R. HE watches her, then moves away, carrying the box and the seeds.)

ELSIE: *(Seeing him, from the"car")* At last . . . hurry, please. I have a dentist appointment in forty-five minutes.

(CHARLIE arrives at the "car.")

GRACE: *(Indicating the box)* What did she give you?

CHARLIE: Personal stuff.

(HE starts to slide into the front seat.)

ELSIE: Mother, ask him to sit in back, please.

GRACE: *(Sliding over, making room)* That's all right, Elsie. We're all in this thing together.

(CHARLIE slides in, sits, holding the box in his lap. They drive. CHARLIE reaches over and turns on the radio. Music comes up loud: a song from 1945 such as "It's Been a Long, Long Time." ELSIE reaches over and turns it off.)

ELSIE: Can't we have some adult conversation?

CHARLIE: *(Turning it on again)* It's a democracy, isn't it? It's a free country.

GRACE: *(Turning it down)* Let's at least not have it quite so loud . . . *(The music continues under more softly.)*

CHARLIE: *(In "car"; to audience)* So I tried photography in boarding school. And took up writing in college. And finally, last summer, I wrote this play.

ELSIE: *(Looking out)* Oh look. There's the Peace Bridge.

GRACE: And the city beyond.

(THEY look. ANNA stands, isolated in her own light, looking out at the lake. The music comes up as the lights fade on all.)

THE END